Book & Page

Flagg Mountain Press
13 Louisburg Square
Centerville, MA 02632

© Copyright 1997 by R. PEASE
ISBN 1-889455-02-4

2nd Printing - 2002

Printed in the United States by Morris Publishing
3212 East Highway 30
Kearney, NE 68847
1-800-650-7888

Home, where is it?

IV

Castiglion Fiorentino is a small village not far from Arezzo in central Italy. It boasts of no famous churches and possesses no renowned art works so tourists are generally unaware of its existence. It is simply one of scores of unimportant towns which one finds all over Tuscany, clusters of stone buildings, many centuries old, most often atop a hill or an igneous outcropping, originally walled and fortified, its streets a maze of narrow passageways and arches and its rooftops a tiered checkerboard of weathered red tiles.

Guido Bussatti was born and raised in Castiglion Fiorentino. His father, Piero, was a woodworker. His mother, known as La Minca, a woman of considerable beauty, was an accomplished seamstress. An older sister, Franca, was the only other member of the family.

Toward the end of World War II Guido made the acquaintance of an American soldier. Lance Bragdon was stationed in a villa outside town and Guido was sent to the villa by his father to pick up a chair that had been broken and needed to be repaired. It was late April and the American was taking advantage of the warm sun in the courtyard. He was lying on a mattress on a table working on a tan.

"*Scusi, Signore,*" Guido said. "I am come for the chair."

The American sat up. He was wearing pants only. The sun had made little difference in the color of his skin. He was a young man, not more than two years older than Guido. His body was lean and trim with only a suggestion of a future roll of lard at his belt. He was sitting on the edge of the mattress.

"Gotcha," he said. "The old dames that own this place acted like we'd committed a federal offense the other night when one of their rickety chairs collapsed."

Six Americans were billeted at the villa. In the course of the war Algerians, Brasilians, Germans, Italians and finally Americans had taken up residence there while the two elderly sisters who owned the thirty-room mansion dedicated themselves to the task of preserving the antiques and paintings and rare books and silverware and imported porcelain and reliquaries which more than a dozen generations of titled ancestors had accumulated.

These two, so timid they wouldn't even travel to Arezzo to go shopping, had defied looters and drunkards, machine guns and bombs, foreigners and countrymen in their unremitting defense of *la roba*...the things.

"Come with me," the American said. "We'll go get the chair."

Guido followed. They entered the villa through a door at ground level and then climbed a flight of stone stairs.

"Cold as a goddamned tomb in this joint," the American said. "Put central heating in here and some decent plumbing and rewire the place and it wouldn't be half bad."

At the end of a long corridor they entered a room that had been stripped of everything but the essentials for sleeping, plus a wide table and some kitchen chairs, one of which lay on its side with a broken leg.

"There's the corpus delicti," said the American, pointing. "One of the ancient dames tried to tell me it was authentic Chippendale. I didn't dare tell her what she was full of. Does it look like Chippendale to you?"

Guido smiled. It was typical of the two sisters not to know the difference between an object of real value and a cheap imitation. Louis Quinze, Verrochio, Sevres, Ghiberti - these were only names to them and they didn't know one from another. Only the

Almighty could reveal how many priceless items they had let go and what rubbish they had clung to in their impenetrable ignorance.

"Is not Chippendale," Guido said. "Is only good country design. And you see. Here. Was already mended another time, but not properly."

"So you can tell the ladies we're innocent. Okay?"

"I will do my best to see that you are returned to favor," Guido replied.

He did not have to go looking for the two sisters. They had watched him come through the gate and talk to the American. They called to him when he was in the corridor again and he was led into a small room next to the kitchen. It was the room where they took their meals. A servant, even older than either of them, nearly deaf and half blind, cooked and cleaned and sent peasants to do the shopping. Sofia could be heard through the swinging door, banging pots and muttering as she prepared the noonday meal.

Guido knew what the sisters wanted. Sure enough, they kept him listening politely to their infinite troubles for half an hour before turning him loose. Without trying to correct their conviction that it was authentic Chippendale, he assured them he could repair the chair so that it would be better than new.

"*Dio solo sa quanto costerà*," they said, virtually in unison...Lord only knows how much it will cost.

Guido told them not to worry about the cost, maybe he could get the American to pay. On that note he escaped.

He wanted to see the American again. From earliest childhood he had been intrigued by stories of life in the United States. One of the first movies he saw was a Western full of Cowboys and Indians. How many of those shows did he attend? For years they were almost the only things to be seen in small town cinemas.

At school, the first chance he got, he began studying English, and by the time he finished the *liceo* he could read and write with considerable proficiency. It was the spoken language in which he knew he was deficient. His teachers, when they could speak English at all, had British accents. The chance to hear an American speaking the language of every day America, now, was too good to be true.

When Guido brought the chair back to the villa, three days later, he found Lance Bragdon in the courtyard another time. This time he was writing a letter, stripped to the waist, still working on a tan, but his fair skin had only grown pinker with exposure to the sun.

"Hey, that was pretty quick," the American said. He had a wide happy smile when he spoke, and when he picked up the chair and turned it over he moved gracefully. He looked like a man who had played many sports and all of them well. "Looks like new," he said. "I can't even see where it was mended."

Guido grinned. "Will not break again," he said. "You can be sure."

He had made the repair himself. Under his father's tutelage he was becoming an expert joiner and cabinet maker. He would not be expected to attend a university. He belonged to the working class and would follow in his father's footsteps. When the war was over there would be work for everyone - at least he hoped so.

"How much do we owe you?" Lance asked.

Guido was unsure how to reply. He didn't know if the American had any Italian money and he knew that he didn't want any scrip.

"You give me what you think is worth," he said.

Lance laughed. "Here we go again," he said. How many times since he'd been in Italy had he dickered with Italians, bartering chocolate or cigarettes or equipment for flasks of wine or cameos or the favors of a woman? "You speak, Joe," was the opening gambit in the South. This young man had put it in politer terms.

"Is there anything you need that I might have?" Lance asked.

Guido hadn't thought of this possibility. Before he could answer, Lance said: "Maybe you could use a pair of GI shoes."

Guido glanced down at the pair of shoes he was wearing, cracked at the bend of the toe, the heels worn away. "Do you have a pair that would fit me?" he asked.

"Follow me," the American said, and a second time they entered the looming villa and were embraced by the damp chill of the place.

In the dormitory, Lance opened a foot locker and got out a new pair of shoes. "Try these," he said.

Guido was embarrassed to take off his shoes. There were holes in his socks. Would the American think less of him for that? He unlaced his worn shoes anyway and then slipped his feet into the rugged, ankle-high army boots. They were a perfect fit. Footwear this good was impossible to come by during the war.

"These are worth much more than the repair of the chair," Guido said.

"Then when we bust another piece of furniture you'll fix it for us without charge." Lance was laughing.

Guido looked around the room. "Nothing I see here," he said, "is going to break unless you put it under a truck."

"So you're ahead. That's okay."

Their eyes met in a way they hadn't before. "Maybe, to make us even," Guido said, "I could show you some of the towns, the country, the churches nearby. Would that interest you?"

"Hey. Great idea. And I have the use of a jeep a couple of times each week. How about, let's see...next Tuesday?"

So the two of them spent a number of days together that spring. Lance was not thrilled by churches or old paintings, but he couldn't get enough of towers and cobbled streets and twisting alleyways. He carried a camera and took innumerable pictures, Often, too, they walked out into the country, following dirt roads high into the hills where they would stop and eat lunch, talking about themselves and what they expected to do with their lives, asking each other questions, sharing the excitement of an emerging friendship with someone both foreign and kindred.

Lance was waiting for orders to move out. The five other men with him had been assigned to a supply depot. No reason was given for the fact that he was left free.

Once, before he was reassigned, he came to the apartment where Guido lived, invited for supper. He arrived, carrying a bag of flour, another of sugar, and a carton of cigarettes for Guido's father.

For Lance, they prepared a meal of *tortellini* in chicken broth, followed by *coniglio*...rabbit, cooked on a spit. There was an enormous bowl of new lettuce seasoned with oregano and basil and parsley, dripping with olive oil from their own *podere*, just enough vinegar added to sharpen the taste. Glasses were kept filled with red wine, full-bodied, an elusive flavor of spice in it somewhere, a live wine that had not been pasturized and in which the Italian sun and the rocky soil of Tuscany seemed still to work.

Guido was happy to be kept busy translating questions and answers, and Lance was delighted to be the center of attention.

Franca had learned enough English to be able to say a few things, but she was slow to understand the replies.

"Do many women dye their hair in America?" she asked.

And Lance replied: "The blondes all become brunettes and the brunettes all try being blondes and the old ladies all get a blue rinse."

No one believed him.

"It's true," he said. You go out for supper in the evening, some place that costs and arm and a leg..."

"What is that...costs arms and legs?'

"I mean it's expensive," Lance said. "The lights are so dim you can't tell what you're eating and there's this blue haze in the air. You look around and every old dame in the place has got a big bush of blue hair."

His good nature and his laugh and his love of exaggeration kept them all smiling.

"*Ho sentito*," Piero said, "*che tutti gli Americani son' Signori. Vero?*"

"My father says he has heard that all Americans are *Signori*. By that he means, they must all be rich. Is it true?"

For a moment, Lance did not reply. "The United States is very rich," he said. "Most Americans expect to own their own home and to have at least one, maybe two, automobiles. In many houses there are two bathrooms and there's enough hot water for everyone to take a bath or shower every day. There's work for nearly everyone who wants to work. But no. Not all Americans are rich. Many are poor."

"Would we be considered poor by Americans?" Guido asked.

Lance was no longer smiling. "I think your family is rich in ways that many Americans would not understand," he said.

Had it been just a polite thing to say? Was it like the other thing he had repeated so many times? "You ever get to the States, come see me, my friend. I'll make sure you don't lack for anything."

Guido was called up for military service before the war was over, but he never saw any action, and the months after the war, when he had to stay in uniform, were a dreary waste of time.

After his discharge, he returned to Castiglion Fiorentino but couldn't wait to leave it behind. How provincial it seemed. How hopelessly sunk in a past from which it would never escape!

There was barely enough work to keep his father busy three days a week and no one could pay on time. Without the small piece of land they owned, the *podere*, where they raised vegetables and kept chickens and rabbits, they would surely have been hard pressed. Too much of Italy lay in ruins and rebuilding was slow to start.

Guido succeeded in obtaining a passport and a tourist visa. He had saved almost enough money for passage. His sister loaned him the balance.

He set off with only a back pack, caught rides to Livorno, found a converted troop ship bound for New York City, and in March, 1947, left Italy behind him, not knowing if he would ever return.

America, for him, was a dream of abundance and well-being. He did not expect to find many Cowboys and Indians, but he was confident that the people would welcome him with open arms, that work would be easy to find, that his tourist visa could be renewed indefinitely, that a new, rewarding period in his life was about to begin.

They steamed into New York at dawn. It was snowing. The Statue of Liberty rose above the water, a gray column of cement, and the Torch of Freedom was lost in a swirling whiteness. The awesome towers of the city, their tops invisible, seemed to thrust upwards to the very gates of heaven.

As Guido walked down the gangplank, an icy wind tore at the thin jacket he was wearing. It was April. In Italy wheat was already high in the fields and Americans there could be taking the sun to get tanned. Was this normal? If April was this intemperate, what would winter be like?

There was Customs to be got through. A fat brute with an incomprehensible southern accent did everything but strip-search Guido, went through his meager belongings, one by one, handling each item with obvious disdain. Was he looking for drugs? Guido had never so much as smoked a cigarette. Did he look like someone who would traffic in heroin?

And when at last he was turned loose and started walking the cavernous streets of lower Manhatten, the wind around the base of the tall buildings nearly knocked him over.

He tried to stop several passers-by, but all evaded him before he could ask directions. One, a hefty gentlman in a gray coat with a velvet collar, pressed a quarter into his hand and hurried around him without trying to hear what Guido was saying.

A distant relative was Assistant Professor at Columbia. Guido planned to surprise him. The address was on Riverside Drive. But where was Riverside Drive?

He stopped in front of a place that seemed to be called The White Tower. It was a place to eat. Not a restaurant. It looked cheap. Perhaps someone inside would be able to tell him how to find Riverside Drive.

He walked in through a glass door and sat on a kind of stool with a plastic seat, the whole thing bolted to the floor. On his right, two men were speaking Yiddish. On his left, at the counter, two others were speaking something that might have been Armenian. A man in a soiled white apron, behind the counter, was yelling at someone out of sight in a language that sounded like Spanish. A minute later, this same person approached Guido and asked: "Wuddlabee?"

Guido hesitated. "I am sorry," he said. "I do not understand."

"Wutchawan? Wutchawan?" the man said, and at last Guido caught on.

"A coffee please," he said.

Instead of black, it was presented to him in a huge mug and was about half milk. Guido tasted it. At least it was hot. But he couldn't help thinking how good an *espresso* would have tasted instead of this malodorous liquid.

"Could you tell me, please," Guido asked, before the man could move away, "how do I get from here to Riverside Drive?"

The men on both sides of him turned then to see who he was. They took in the backpack and the tight pants and the worn jacket, the wiry slight build, the accent, the regular features, clean shaven but where a heavy beard was evident even in so young a man.

"Fresh off the ship, right?" It was the man nearest him who asked, the one who had been speaking Yiddish.

"How did you know?" Guido asked.

"Italian, right?"

"Yes, but..."

"An' you gotta relatiff liffs on Riverside Drive."

"Do you see into the future, too?"

The heavy lugubrious Jewish face almost smiled. "You vant I should be telling you also the future?"

Guido shook his head. "That would be dangerous, wouldn't

it," he said.

"Hah. You are a sharp one. But you would not belief vat I would tell you. Not to worry."

"Then could you tell me how to get to Riverside Drive?"

"Grab a taxi. Giff the address. Half an hour, you're there."

"Would that not be expensive?"

The man behind the counter had been listening. Now he snorted. "Snot a Wop," he said. "Sanudda Chew."

The older man Guido had been talking to, and his companion, gave the counterman a venomous look.

"You are short of cash, take the bus. I vill show you the corner. But finish first your coffee." Old eyes had crinkled almost shut. Ear lobes, detached and pendulous, trembled against the man's coat collar. His skin was the same color as the cement sidewalk outside, but from somewhere within him came a warmth Guido could all but feel against cheek.

The two who might have been Armenian were talking again. The one behind the counter went back to yelling at someone in a room behind him.

"That you are coming, does your relatif know?"

"Nobody knows that I am in America now," Guido said.

"Perhaps you should telephone. Be sure somebody iss home. From here iss a long ride to Riverside Drive."

"I would rather surprise," Guido said.

"This iss a close relatif?"

"No. Is a cousin of my father."

Through slits the width of a thumbnail the old man was watching Guido. "Then maybe you are right," he said. "To phone can be mistake. On the phone one says easily: 'Vat a pity! For Connecticut ve vas chust leaffing.'"

Guido sensed that there might be some truth in this. He finished as much of the so-called coffee as he could, then buttoned his jacket again.

The older man walked him to the bus stop and stayed with Guido until the bus came. He was still standing there as the huge vehicle pulled away. Was he seeing himself some decades earlier, Guido wondered. Had he, too, come to New York alone - from Russia, in his case, from Hungary, from Poland? Had this proven to be a land of opportunity for him?

The sun came out. Where snow flurries had left tailings an hour before, the streets gleamed black and shiny, wet for a moment, soon to be dry. People leaned into the wind. Papers and wrappers spun in miniature tornadoes.

On the sidewalks, at crossings, aboard the bus, men and women everywhere moved or stood, intent on what they were doing. None spoke to the others near them. Did no one go out with a friend, a parent, a child, a spouse? Was each and every one alone?

A woman in a gray suit and a copper-green hat got on with three other people. While the others deposited the correct change in the meter, she appeared to be seeking in her purse for the necessary coins. The bus started up and went four blocks before someone rang for it to stop.

"Hey. You wit da green hat," the driver said, loud enough for all to hear. "Ya gonna pay, or ya gonna get off?"

Still fumbling in her satchel, the woman moved slowly back toward the door. "I must have left my money at home," she said resignedly.

"Yeah, sure. Every time ya go out, I bet," the driver said.

Guido sought the eyes of the other passengers, but eye contact did not seem to exist. Not a person within earshot was unaware of what was happening, yet without exception, each was pretending to be absorbed in looking out the window, or examining a parcel, or reading a folded newspaper. The sarcastic, abrasive tone of the driver was enough to raise anyone's hackles. In Italy, a similar scene would have split the occupants of the bus into two factions immediately, all with an opinion to be loudly enunciated. Someone would have made the grand gesture of paying the lady's fare to the cheers of the believers and the hoots of the doubters. These New Yorkers, though, were impervious. Did they know something he didn't know? The lady stepped down from the bus and the door banged shut behind her.

Because he could not be sure of the numbers, Guido got off the bus several blocks before reaching the address he wanted. It didn't matter. This way he had a chance to look at another section of the city.

He found it hard to believe that so many enormous buildings could all be divided into separate quarters. The entire population of Castiglion Fiorentino could have moved into just one of the vast apartment complexes he passed. Did generations of living in only two or three rooms, in buildings occupied by countless others, most of the rooms without windows or with views only of walls and air shafts - did this change people? Did genetic differentiation take place? Was this part of what kept two human beings from looking at one another in a crowd? "Don't speak to strangers." You tell a child that. So you are bumped into, jostled at a crossing or on a bus. It's impersonal. You have your invisible chitin about you. Your protective shield. You have not felt the touch of a human hand, heard a human voice, exchanged a look. You are safe.

For half an hour Guido wondered if he would ever find the address he was seeking. Just getting from one number to the next meant walking as far as from his home to the nearest shop in Castiglione.

When he did find the number he wanted, he was in for another surprise.

Dott. Attilio Ronchetti, the card read. So this was where his uncle lived. But more than seventy other names were listed at the same number. And what names they were! Colopy, Sigle, Blue,

Garabedian. O, Hrubi, Beetle, Zychowicz, Undergarter, Panagiatacopoulos, Slaughter, Shchelokov, Dinkeloo, Wiinekainen, Chaio, Zeltner, Agarwal, Mertelsmann, Abdul-Qader, Her, Takagi, Itil, Pixley, Klotsky...Where were the Americans? Was this America? Could these all be hospital staff, university professors, foreign professionals all gathered into one place by choice or by segregation? Surely a substantial income was required if one could live in this neighborhood. But what had become of Smith and Jones and Brown?

Guido pushed the button next to the name of his father's cousin. There was no response. He pushed again and held the contact for several seconds.

It was eleven A. M. Apparently, no one was in. Attilio was married and his wife's name was Fulvia. Shouldn't a wife be at home? But maybe she, too, had a job. Then when would either one return? And suppose they had gone to - where did the old Jewish man say - Connecticut?

A woman in her sixties came into the foyer. She had a key in her hand. Before Guido could think of a question to ask her, she had unlocked the plate glass door and gone into the main entrance and the lock had clicked shut again. Only then did she take a long look at Guido, not meeting his eyes, but examining him from head to toe through the glass.

Moments after she had disappeared, a man in a three-quarter length leather jacket, hands in side pockets, appeared beside Guido.

"You looking for someone?" he asked.

"I am come to visit Mr. Ronchetti," Guido answered.

"You rung the bell?"

"Yes. There was no answer."

"So he ain't to home."

"Do you know when he will come home?"

"You kiddin?"

Guido was puzzled. "Kiddin?" he repeated. "Is small cat, no? I do not understand."

"Some kinda wise guy, are ya?" The man moved a step closer. "You better move along, wise guy. Nobody loiters here."

This one was looking straight at him. The flesh around his eyes was puffed out and fatty so that the small brown orbs were nearly hidden, but the menace in them was unmistakable.

"Mr. Ronchetti is my uncle," Guido said, not knowing how else to explain the relationship.

"He expecting you?"

"No. My boat just docked a couple of hours ago."

"So he don' know yer comin'. Maybe he don' even know you. Maybe he ain' even yer uncle. You could maybe be waitin' to get inside an' rip off somebody's pad." The man moved another step closer. His belly was almost touching Guido's jacket.

"Out," the man said. "Move it. I catch you hangin' around here again, I call the cops."

Guido was forced outside. It was raining, but before he had walked three blocks the sun returned.

An elderly man, walking a Golden Retriever, told him how to get to Columbia University. It was not too far to walk. Once there, Guido kept asking until someone got on a phone and called Administration. Professor Ronchetti was in a seminar at the moment but would be free at the end of the hour. A black student from Nigeria led Guido to a building and then upstairs to a hall where Guido could wait for the class to be over.

The black man, who looked like a pugilist, was studying Sociology, he said. He was a prince in his own land, but here he was little better than a servant. He would return home, though, in three years, if all went well, and rule.

- Three years, Guido thought. And where will I be in three years?

When the classroom door finally opened and the students

trooped out, Guido went in and found his uncle slipping papers into a leather briefcase with fine Florentine designs on it.

The professor looked up. There was no sign of recognition in his eyes.

"Yes?" he said.

"*Sono Guido Bussatti*...I am Guido Bussatti. I didn't think you would recognize me."

His uncle was staring at him now. "*Guido. Guido? Mica possibile. Eppure*...Guido. Guido? It's not possible. And yet...You are Piero's son. Isn't that so?"

"I only got to New York this morning."

"And you managed to find your way here?"

"A man in a black leather coat at your house on Riverside Drive said he would call the police if I waited there."

Guido had imagined his uncle would embrace him when they met. It didn't happen. They shook hands instead.

"This is indeed a surprise," the uncle said, then added: "And a pleasure. I want to hear all about Piero and..." he had forgotten their names... "the rest of the family. And my poor Italy. And what brings you here. Come. I'm through for the day. We'll go back to the apartment."

Ronchetti was a tall spare man. He stood straight, head held high and shoulders back. His hair was fine and fair, but it was thin on top. Long tapering fingers held the briefcase. His three-piece suit was tailor-made. There was a determined look of aristocracy about him.

Guido was aware of their contrasting appearance. Was that why his uncle seemed in a hurry to get away from the university? This erect, talkative man was chattering on about the ravages of war, the new species of student descending upon the university, the difficulty of making a salary suffice in New York City. He asked questions and then didn't wait to hear the answers.

They got into a gleaming new four-door Fiat and in minutes

were parked underground within the apartment building which Guido had only seen from the foyer. There was no sign of the belligerent guard. An elevator, that rose like a rocket, took them to a windowless corridor. Ronchetti used two different keys to open the door to his apartment.

"We had to wait more than a year to get in here," Ronchetti said. "Finding any kind of place to live near the university is a major task."

There was a kind of apology in his uncle's words. Maybe he understood that Guido would think the apartment small. And it was. Even Guido, several inches shorter than his uncle, could have touched the ceilings without stretching. The livingroom and the bedroom were of minimal proportions. There was a very efficient-looking kitchen, and there was a sparkling bathroom, perhaps the most impressive room of all. In Guido's *quartiere* in Castiglione, which was ten times as large as this apartment, the *gabinetto* was a tiny cold corner as distant from all other rooms as possible. Americans had different priorities, it seemed.

"So you decided to come to the United States for a little visit? Is that it?"

Ronchetti had taken off hat and coat. He sat in a large easy chair and gestured to Guido to make himself comfortable. For the first time, he waited for a reply. Was there some anxiety in his voice?

Guido set his backpack on the floor and sank into a chair opposite his uncle. "I have a friend in Massachusetts," he said. "I'm going to see him. And then..."

"A friend in Massachusetts! Wonderful! How did you get to know him? But of course. It was some American soldier. Maybe you helped him with a little black market at the end of the war. Yes?"

Guido would have denied it, but his uncle was already lecturing again - the corrupting influences of warfare, the demoralization of occupied nations, the ingenuity of the average Italian. Was black market dealing a virtue then? Guido could make little sense of all this palaver. It was clear that his uncle was not much interested in him as long as he was going to be moving on.

The strange thing was, that his uncle continued to speak English. In part, Guido was happy to hear as much of this language as possible, but he knew his own speech was halting, that it put him at a disadvantage. There were things he would like to have said, but obviously he was not going to be given the chance.

When Fulvia came in it was almost two o'clock. Guido could still feel the boat moving under him and he was dizzy with hunger.

"*Molto piacere, Signora*," Guido said when he was introduced. But Fulvia, too, would speak only in English. What was this insistence on using a foreign language when they were all three Italians? It was not as if he came from Avellino and spoke a southern dialect. But maybe that did have something to do with it. They wanted to put a certain distance between themselves and their country of origin. There was something a little bit lower-class about being Italian and these two did not want to be mistaken for peasants or poor immigrants.

Fortunately, Fulvia was hungry. She was director of a clinic for autistic children and worked from eight to one. She went without breakfast to keep her figure, she said, and came home famished those four days a week that she went to her office.

The few minutes that Attilio spent washing up in the bathroom were enough for Fulvia, busy fixing lunch, to make polite inquiries about Guido's parents and sister, to learn that he was headed for Massachusetts, and to impress upon him what a full life they led. She was efficient and courteous, but if there was any human warmth in her it was artfully concealed. No doubt she was capable of controlled anger, but affection? Love?

Guido learned that a BLT was a bacon, lettuce and tomato

sandwich. It was not his idea of a meal. The white bread was about as substantial as a mouthful of fog. The mayonnaise was something frothy and artificial. The tomato could have been a cold potato except for its pale pink color. But he was too hungry to let it matter. The bacon was new to him and made him so thirsty he rather enjoyed the milk, which would have been anathema in Italy. Even the Oreos, he dispatched without undue repugnance.

He couldn't help wondering why Fulvia was worried about maintaining her figure. She was too thin, by his standards. She was almost as tall as her husband. Her angular bony frame was not without a certain severe and commanding aura of authority. One could easily see how she would run her office, brooking no equivocation. Did she deal with the children? That was more difficult to imagine.

They ate their sandwiches at a formica table in the kitchenette. Everything was immaculate. In the wall cabinets, every plate and glass had its precise place. Every utensil used, disappeared into the double sink the minute it was no longer needed. A plant, in a terra cotta bowl, hanging from the ceiling in one corner, was the only decorative addition.

At least in the livingroom there were a few personal touches. Most of one wall there was bookshelves. Guido had noticed that his uncle's field, the *Rinascimento*, was well represented. And Dickens was there, and Moravia and Italo Svevo. He didn't know who C. P. Snow was, or Claudel or Camus, or Gunter Grass. The only Americans he saw were Faulkner and Updike. Those names were familiar. There were lots of Art books. And History. But did his uncle and his wife still read? Had they read for their own pleasure once, as he had done so often. Their library had a studied look. Where were the paperbacks and the whodunits, or the science fiction? How come Attilio and Fulvia had no books that were just fun?

Besides the sofa and chairs and an impressive inlaid *scrivania*...a desk that certainly had come from Italy, there was one piece of modern sculpture in the room. And there was a painting which was signed Rosai. It showed a workman in a blue coverall looking out at the viewer from a darkness, ill at ease. How did that get here? Maybe it was bought as an investment?

"Well, then," Fulvia said, when they were having coffee (real coffee, *se Dio vuole*, Guido thought). "So you will be going to visit your friend. In what town does he live?"

"He comes from Billerica," Guido said, pronouncing it all wrong. Not until he got there would he discover its idiosyncratic pronunciation.

"Is that near Boston?"

"Is a little way north of Boston," Guido said.

"Let's see if we can find it on the map." Fulvia went into the bedroom and came back with a road map. "We took a trip to Maine last year," she said, "so I still have a record of where we went. Let's see...north of Boston. Here it is. But how do you expect to get there?"

"I thought I would try - how do you say - bumming?"

There was no comment on that. Guido sensed he had said something he shouldn't have. But this was America and Lance had told him that thousands of young men made it from one place to another all the time, simply by getting onto the highway and sticking out a thumb. Evidently Attilio and Fulvia didn't approve. Probably they had never given a ride to anyone, either.

"You better take the map, in that case," Fulvia said. "This one covers all of New England. You'll want to stay on the major highways, I think. It wouldn't be wise to get lost."

- And what would be so unwise about being lost, Guido thought. Are only the main roads the safe ones? Isn't it by exploring, by getting onto the back ways that I will learn something of this country? But that wasn't what Fulvia had had in mind. She had been saying something else. As she handed him the map he got the feeling she couldn't wait to have him out of the apartment.

Then she and Attilio exchanged a look. Perhaps they realized how inhospitably they were behaving.

"But you don't have to be rushing off now," Attilio said. "You will spend the night here. We'll get to know each other. Tomorrow I can drive you to a place from which to start your journey."

Guido was embarrassed. He was sure they would have been glad to see him walk out right then. Where was he going to sleep? But having offered him welcome for the night, they had cornered themselves. They couldn't decently let him leave.

An Italian phrase came to mind: *Levo l'incomodo*...I will remove the inconvenience. He was tempted to say it. At the same time, he had no idea how he would manage if he had to start looking for a way out of New York at this time in the afternoon. A bath, maybe a meal, a night's sleep - then he would be ready for anything. And his uncle had said he would take him to a good starting place.

"I'm very grateful to you," he said. "I know that coming here is an imposition. Thank you."

"So that's settled." Attilio gave his wife another look. He turned back to Guido. "Now tell us what is happening in Italy."

But, of course, Guido never got the chance. His uncle was not a listener. Then the phone rang. Later, Fulvia needed to do some shopping for supper. Conversation, what there was of it, was desultory. Attilio had some paper work to get out of the way. That occupied him for an hour.

The evening meal was lively enough. Fulvia sautéed some chicken - those soft white-fleshed American chickens - and served it with a green salad and Lebanese bread. The red wine was adequate. She had chocolate ice cream for dessert. That was good.

When it was time for bed, they took turns in the refulgent bathroom, that monument to bodily functions. Guido could scarcely believe the tremendous gush of scalding water that poured into the emerald-green tub when he touched the faucet.

While he was bathing, Fulvia transformed the livingroom sofa into a bed. By ten-thirty all the lights were out.

Guido lay in the almost dark. Sleep was not going to come soon. He was tired but tense. As his eyes adjusted, he could make out the dim shapes of the big armchairs and he could feel the look of Rosai's giant laborer on him.

He wondered where the light came from. The only window in the room looked out on a blank wall. There must have been some light in the sky, the million lights of the city reflected back down out of the dust-filled dome of heaven.

On the ship he had slept like a baby. The ocean's motion, even the two days when a storm battered them and other passengers were ill, had pleased him, soothed him. And the salt air and the wind and the immensity of the sky had all seemed familiar, like parts of a life he had known but not recently remembered.

This steel and cement enclosure, this assemblage of cells with its countless occupants, was alien to him. The air was strange. No window was open. Could one then suffocate? And in what should have been quiet, he made out a ceaseless dull rumble and mutter of distant traffic, subways, planes; and closer, the hiss and the gurgle and whisper of pumps, fans, motors, toilets flushing, perhaps even human voices distorted and lowered in their passage through girders and ductwork and grimy windows.

The great stillness of the country did not exist here. At night, in Castiglion Fiorentino, when the silence was broken, whatever the noise, it was isolated and distinct, and for hours on end, more often than not, there was no sound, only a spreading black velvet blanket of quiet.

In the morning, after making separate offerings at the ceramic altar, after showers and shaves and breakfast (of a sort), Guido said goodbye to Fulvia and then his uncle drove him to a place where he might be able to get a ride.

It was a ramp onto a highway. Cars were streaming by going into the city. Very few came down the ramp to head out of the city into the east and northeast. Guido was self-conscious about putting up his thumb in what he hoped was the right gesture. A dozen vehicles shot past him without a glance. When one swerved to a stop next to him, he hardly knew what to do. The door swung open. "Jump in quick," the driver yelled, his eye on the rear-view mirror to be sure no one was about to ram him from behind. Guido jumped in and the car took off as he closed the door.

"How far you goin'?"

"I hope to get to a place just north of Boston." Guido said.

"No sweat. I'll get you well on your way."

The driver was a black man, compact, muscular. He might have been any age in the middle years. He handled the driving with ease. The car could have been a part of him, so naturally did it respond to his touch.

"Are you returning to school," he asked.

"No. I go to see a friend. I have just come from Italy."

"How about that! *La bell'Italia*. What part of Italy?"

"I am from Tuscany."

"Lucky guy. I was based in southern Italy for a year and when the war was over I managed to get a week in Florence. Terrible destruction there. Senseless. Like all of warfare. But the countryside! Those hills! Fiesole! The Piazzale Michelangelo! You know, there was a sense of timelessness about all that region. Things that had continued unchanged for ever and ever. I've often thought how wonderful it would be to return there."

"We could change places," Guido said, smiling.

The black man turned to look at him, an intent look that asked questions Guido could not have put into words. Then he, too, smiled, a huge white-toothed smile full of pleasure. "It should be that easy," he said. Then he stuck out his right hand. "They call me Flyin' Fingers," he said. "I play the piano."

Guido took his hand. It was warm and strong. They shook.

"What do they call you?" the man asked.

"I am Guido Bussatti."

"Guido Bussatti. I'll remember that. I never forget a name or a face. Will the world be hearing from you, Guido Bussatti?"

"Is not likely," Guido said. "I am only a *falegname*...a carpenter, a joiner, a woodworker you would say."

"Better honest than famous." There was a note of something like regret in the man's voice.

"And you, Mr. Flyin' Fingers," Guido asked, "has the world already heard from you?"

"They better hear pretty soon. Time's beginnin' to run out."

"You are older than you look?"

"I'm fifty-two, Friend." The laughter had left his voice. He was staring down the road ahead of him, miles ticking away beneath the swift-moving automobile. "Things are changin' now," he said. "Black musicians can play more places than they used to. The clubs treat us better. On the road, though, you never know what kinda shit some hotel-keeper, barman, restaurant-owner gonna throw at you."

"I would like to hear you play."

"You like good jazz?"

"Very much."

"Who you like on piano?"

"I've listened to records with Jess Stacy, Johnny Guarnieri, Teddy Wilson, Bud Powell. Is it like some of them you play?"

"You put me in excellent company."

"I must hear you. I think good jazz is an expression of joy. When jazz is really good, is like fresh spring water when you are thirsty."

"If you hear me someday," the driver said, "I'll try not to disappoint you."

East of New Haven, Guido was a long time getting a second ride. He walked for a couple of miles trying to locate a spot where traffic might slow down. None appeared.

Eventually, an old Plymouth with a crumpled fender pulled over. The driver was overweight, nearly bald. The back seat was completely filled with small boxes.

"You want a ride?"

"Thank you," Guido said, as he got in.

The car started up again and drew out into traffic. "I'm going to Providence. Is that on your way?"

Guido looked at his map and found Providence. "That's very good," he said. "I started in New York City this morning, and in two rides I'll be almost to Boston."

"We're not to Providence yet, though. It's a good two hours and we might stop on the way. You in a hurry?"

"No hurry," Guido replied.

"On vacation?"

"Is a vacation, in a way."

"Something about the way you talk...the accent. Not Puerto Rican, are you?"

"I am Italian."

"*Paesan*, eh?"

"I come from Tuscany."

"It's all the same country, Pal."

"Italy is many countries," Guido said.

"First time I ever heard that."

"What I mean to say is, there are great differences among Italians from different parts of Italy."

"Yeah, I suppose you're right. But an Eye-tie is an Eye-tie. Right?"

"I guess you could say that."

Guido did not think that pursuing this subject would get them anywhere. He looked at the countryside they were passing through, the huge trees and the rolling meadows, the land just beginning to show green here and there, a hollow the sun hadn't reached where snow still lay. When they passed through a town, he marveled to see that all the houses were built of wood. Only public buildings were made of brick or stone.

The old car was traveling at about forty miles per hour. Each time it accelerated it left a cloud of black smoke behind it. Other cars passed them continually.

Guido felt something touch his thigh. It was the driver's right hand.

"Are you mad at me because I called you an Eye-tie?" the man asked.

"I think you should keep your hand on the driving wheel."

"The driving wheel is here," the man said, fingers moving up Guido's leg.

"I mean it." Guido said.

Their eyes met then and the driver removed his hand. He looked back at the road, drove in silence for a minute or two, then pulled over onto the grass.

"You can walk from here," he said. Tears were running from his eyes. Guido got out. He didn't know how to say anything. He slammed the door and the car took off and disappeared down the highway.

"*Un finocchio*," Guido said aloud.

He was troubled without knowing why. Perhaps the sight of a grown man crying had shaken him. He tried to imagine what sort of life such an aging homosexual might have. Was he a man who had tried marriage and who had not been able to make it work? Did he have children? Something about his defeated look made Guido think he might have struggled with marriage for many years before finally giving up. Now he traveled with his load of samples, or toys, or souvenirs - whatever it was in all the boxes in the back seat - and he had to settle for sex by the wayside, sex with strangers. He was unprepossessing, repugnant physically. But he still had feelings. He wept when rejected.

Guido took a deep breath and exhaled strenuously as if to cleanse himself of stale air.

The grass he stood on was showing new growth and there was a smell of earth warming under the sun. A hawk that had been perched on a dead limb ahead of Guido leaned forward just when Guido noticed him and sailed across the road into a stand of oak. It had wide rounded wings and a short ruddy fan-shaped tail. A band of black streaks divided its white underparts in two.

For a while, Guido walked again, not that he was looking for a better spot from which to get a ride. He just felt like walking. He would have kept on longer, but a medium-sized truck stopped beside him. "If you want a lift, hop in," said the young man who was driving.

Guido climbed up onto the seat. The truck was old and seemed to be carrying a heavy load.

"Got everything I own in this old ark," the driver said. "If she breaks down before I get to Wellfleet I'll be glad to have someone along to help."

The fellow was wiry and high strung. He had on a black turtleneck sweater and blue jeans. Brown wavy hair grew long over his forehead and down the back of his neck. His hands moved on the wheel, patting it, sliding around and back continually.

"Gonna start a new life," he said. "Lived in two rooms in Hartford for three years. Worked my ass off. Two jobs. The wife always yappin' at me the minute I was home. The kid screamin'. Never could get any sleep. Lucky to get a piece of tail once a week. Nothin' but aggravation. I told her: 'You gonna get off my back or am I gonna walk out?' She never quit yappin' long enough to hear me. So I borrowed this ole barn-on-wheels an' I loaded all the furniture I paid for along with a load of lumber I got from a guy in bankruptcy, all my ole tools too, an' I'm gonna go live in Wellfleet. Was there once eight years ago. I'll find some place to hole up. I'll do building. I'll go fishin'. I'll live off the land and live alone. No way will I ever get hitched again."

Guido tried to take it all in. It was not easy. How could a man no older than he was, be starting a new life? And what would become of the wife and child he was leaving in some place called Heartford? He got out his map and found Hartford. Was that the same place? Then he looked for Wellfleet. Where could that be?

"What you looking for? Wellfleet? It's way out on Cape Cod. That map won't show it. Unless there's an insert. Where you goin'?"

Guido spoke for the first time. "I'm going to a place just north of Boston," he said.

"So I'll drop you off at the Sagamore Bridge. Right here." He put a finger on the spot on the map without slowing down. "You'll only be an hour or two from Boston then. You married?"

Guido said that he wasn't.

The fellow was off again on the subject - everything that was wrong with marriage. He was obsessed with it. Unless he filled his life with something new he'd soon begin to miss what he most railed against.

It was barely one o'clock when Guido got down from the truck at the Sagamore Bridge. He walked around the rotary to the side headed north and almost immediately got picked up by a car with three older women in it. They were going to Boston on a shopping spree, a formidable trio, non-stop talkers, grandmothers all, chairpersons every one of a committe on Women's Rights, or Organized Revolt against Drinking and Driving, or Peace Through Love.

They found out more about Guido in one hour than anyone but his own mother had ever known. They gave him advice on everything under the sun except how to handle homosexual advances. They had the answers and the keys to all the major and minor troubles of the world. In a combined total of almost two hundred years they had buried five husbands and had not finished their work by any means. A sempiternal, indestructible triumvirate, their self-assurance and basic goodness were shield against all possible doubt or encroachment.

Guido had never encountered anything resembling them before. A hamper they had brought with them contained smoked oysters, ham, potato salad, French pâtisseries, coffee and hot chocolate. Guido was not permitted to refuse anything offered to him. When he could eat no more, they gave him a wool scarf because they knew he would be cold when night came on, and when they found out where he was going, they drove to the other side of Boston and set him on the right road before waving goodbye and resuming their planned assault on Filene's and Bonwit Teller and Shreve, Crump and Low.

The last leg of his journey was the slowest. It took four separate rides and a long walk before Guido found the address Lance had given him two years before.

He walked up to a big old three-story house. A Mrs. Bragdon came to the door after he rang, but she was Lance's mother. She said Lance was married now and lived in his own home. She didn't ask Guido in. She gave him the new address and told him how to get there and then closed the door.

He had another long walk across town, part of the same route he had already traveled, and at last found the street.

Tract houses on miniscule lots ran down both sides. Number 31 was near the next corner. There were no trees. The developer had leveled everything and then had planted his two-bedroom-and-bath ranches in a straight line.

Guido pushed a button and heard chimes sound inside the house. He waited. The door opened. Lance stood before him. His friend had put on thirty pounds or more. He needed a shave. He looked at Guido blankly for a full half minute before recognizing him.

"Hey. It's you. Guido. How ya doin', Man? Come on in."

Guido entered a livingroom full of overstuffed chairs and coffee tables. A huge sofa was against one wall with sections of a newspaper strewn over it and onto the floor. Lance was in his stocking feet. The two muddy work boots, one by the sofa, the other half way across the rug, had to be his. A floor lamp with the shade akimbo threw crazy shadows against the walls.

"So ya decided to come to the States after all," Lance said. "Not enough doin' in Itly, eh?" That was the way he pronounced it, without the 'a.' Guido had forgotten that.

"Hey, Hun," Lance yelled. "Come on in here."

A thin girl, she looked about nineteen, came into the room from what was evidently the kitchen. She had a baby on one hip.

"This is my pal Guido I told you about," Lance said. "Sal, my wife. And the heir to the throne, Lance Junior."

Sal's arms were busy with the baby so she couldn't shake hands. Guido bowed slightly and said: "I'm pleased to meet you, Mrs. Bragdon. This is a nice surprise."

"Yeah. We kinda had to marry up fast," Lance said. "Ya know how it is."

"Oh Lance," Sal protested. "You don't always have to say that."

"Hey, this is Guido, Baby. Nothin' but straight talk with my old buddy. How about a beer, Old Buddy?"

Before Guido could say he'd prefer plain water, Lance went to the kitchen and reappeared with an opened bottle. He already had one of his own.

"So you'll stay for supper and we can shoot the breeze about the good old days in Itly."

Sal gave her husband a look of pleading but he ignored it. The baby began to whine. Sal returned to the kitchen.

"How long ya been on this side of the Atlantic?" Lance asked. "Ya shoulda looked me up right away."

"As a matter of fact, that's what I did. I just got to New York yesterday morning. I spent the first night with an uncle there and today I have come here."

Lance seemed a bit taken aback. He raised his bottle and drank deeply.

Guido had tried to guess what it would be like finding his friend again. He had expected a greater show of warmth and had hoped for a place to stay while he decided what he wanted to do. He had to find some kind of work quickly. Lance had said he would help. Would he? Could he? There was a battered pick-up truck in the carport outside. That could mean that Lance was working, but this tacky little house did not look prosperous.

"How long you expect to be in the States?" Lance asked.

"I have a visa for three months, but I count on getting it renewed. Who knows? I think a year would be enough to find out if I want to stay longer."

Guido could feel a change in the air, or in the quality of the look Lance gave him. Something had altered. In Italy, toward the end of the war, they had offered each other equal shares of discovery of new areas. Lance had been able to talk about aspects of America which Guido was eager to understand. And Guido had had access to people and places and customs in Italy which Lance would not otherwise have found. Each had been able to give freely.

Was one more in debt than the other? Did Guido have the right to remind Lance of the offers he had made? But just his being here was a reminder.

Like a lover who has sworn undying adoration and who is later faced with practical realities, Lance was probably realizing that promises made in the euphoria of emerging friendship were about to be called to account.

"Tell me what you are doing," Guido said, in order to break the awkward silence.

Lance put his feet on a low table in front of him and crossed his legs at the ankles. "I been framin' houses with a guy I know. The winter was tough. We lost a lotta time because of lousy weather. It's pickin' up now. There should be steady work for the next six months."

He had plans to buy some land and become a developer himself. Ten per cent down would get him started. He just needed that and enough to get one house built. Everything was on credit. Hustle was the secret. If you moved fast enough things pyramided. The demand for houses was greater than anyone could satisfy.

What he wanted was to get his mother to mortgage the big house in town. If he could only get her to go along with him he'd be off and flying.

"But she can't understand what's goin' on," Lance said. "It's like talkin' to a bag of cement. There she is, livin' all alone in that old barn that's worth a bundle. It's free and clear and she won't ask for a loan on it. I told her: 'Ma, the money you borrow today you don't pay back until maybe ten years from now. With the way inflation is goin', you may wind up payin' back only half of what you borrow.' Do you think she can grab that? Jesus!"

He was still lamenting his mother's stubborn refusal to understand his needs when Sal came in to say supper was ready.

They ate in an alcove off the kitchen. The baby was in a high chair and Sal was kept busy trying to get him to eat something that came out of a jar and looked like dog vomit.

There was white bread and a butter dish on the table. Three plates held servings of canned spaghetti, a boiled hot dog and canned peas on top of it. Lance seemed to expect nothing better. He ate hungrily and mopped up his plate with part of a slice of the abominable bread.

Guido did his best to swallow what was before him. He could not remember ever eating anything worse than the canned spaghetti. The mustard the others used on the hot dog seemed to help, but he wondered what would happen to his insides in the night. A blueberry pie, and milk, unless he wanted more beer, completed the meal. If American pastry was all as bad as that poisonous blue syrup in the lard-heavy flaky crust, he would never want to try it again.

Lance's wife had just about nothing to say. To Guido, she seemed thin and worn out, defeated before she had even started to live. She cleared the table, as soon as all of them had finished eating, stacked everything in the sink and then took the baby into what must have been the bedroom.

Lance put his elbows on the table and looked at Guido. "So that's how it is, Old Buddy." he said.

What did he mean? You've seen it all? That's my life now?

Somehow, Guido did not think there would be much improvement in his friend's life as the years went by. Did Lance understand that? Was that what Lance was saying?

In Italy, for a great many generations, peasants had lived on land owned by others. Guido had spent some time in the south and remembered hearing an old man say *servo suo* to his master, the land owner...your servant? No, it was stronger than that. It meant, your serf. And there were a thousand years of acceptance of this condition. But the peasants, the *contadini*, were no longer as resigned as they had once been. They were uneasy in the role they had accepted, in many cases, from as far back as the Middle

Ages.

Guido, not a peasant, but only a notch higher on the social scale, had felt the same restlessness that was stirring all over Italy and had come to America, not like those who had immigrated at the turn of the century, fleeing insufferable poverty, but as one impelled to seek and expect a fuller existence.

And here was Lance, the very symbol of the exuberance and optimism which had brought Guido to the States, suddenly reduced to saying: "So that's how it is." Lance, gone fat and soft. Lance, who could eat canned spaghetti without realizing it was something even the poorest Italian would refuse. Lance, already beaten, resigned to mediocrity, ready to blame his mother for not getting his chance.

Guido couldn't wait to get away. He had not traveled five thousand miles for this.

"Do you know where I can find a cheap place to stay?" he asked.

Lance rubbed his chin with his right hand. The sandpapery scratch of his beard on his rough palm mingled with the hum of the refrigerator and the hiss of the fluorescent light overhead.

"There's a rooming house in town that's not bad," he said. Suddenly he, too, couldn't seem to wait to put an end to their reunion.

They went out together without trying to say goodbye to Sal, who was in the bathroom with the baby. They got into the old truck. Lance drove for five minutes in silence.

The rooming house was another solid three-story structure built, probably, about the turn of the century. The woman who ran it said there was a room on the second floor, next to a shared bathroom, for six-fifty a week. Guido would be allowed to cook in his room. He took it.

Lance stuck out his hand. "Great to see you again," he said. "Come by later in the week and let us know how you make out."

Guido shook his friend's hand. He didn't ask where he should start looking to find work. "Thank you," he said. "And tell your wife thanks for supper."

These were things you said, he realized. Was it any different in any other part of the world? You clothed boredom or disgust, disappointment or relief, in words that had a familiar sound but meant nothing. Polite. Vague. A way to get through the moment.

When Lance was gone, Guido went upstairs to his room. There was an ugly iron bed in it and one easy chair, a table of sorts with a lamp on it, a refrigerator that looked older than the house and a single gas burner on an improvised shelf. Flowered curtains hung at the one window. There was linoleum on the floor. On the back of the door was a list of rules: No visitors and no radios after 10 PM. NO pets. RENT must be paid in advance each week ON TIME.

Guido used the bathroom. It was clean. Then he returned to his room and locked the door. He took paper and pen from his backpack and sat at the table where other roomers had eaten sandwiches and soup and whatever other things transients and single persons would eat in a place of this sort.

"*Carissimi*," he wrote, "*sono in America da due giorni*...Dearest ones, I have been in America for two days. This is a land of contrasts. In New York City I saw automobiles that must have cost as much as a whole villa in Florence and on the sidewalk where they passed were men so poor they wore newspapers wrapped around their legs to keep them warm.

"On one corner, where I waited, for ten minutes I did not hear a single person speak a word of English. Italian either. But they tell me New York is the biggest Italian city in the world, has more Italians than Rome or Milan. I didn't see them.

"The streets, near where the boat docked, were like caverns, narrow and dark, with the stone buildings, their tops actually lost in the clouds, leaning over them forbiddingly.

"Uncle Attilio let me spend the first night with him and his wife. Their apartment is very nice and they are both quite successful, but you would almost not know that they come from Italy. They send their 'regards' to all of you.

"On the road I met some very different types of people. There was no trouble getting rides, as there is in Italy. Americans are either terribly suspicious, seeing a thief or an evil person in everyone, or they are so friendly they seem foolish.

"Outside New York I traveled through many small towns and some larger ones. The small towns are often tranquil tasteful places where one might live quietly in pleasant surroundings. There are many stretches of open country too - rolling pastures, meadows, woodlands, tall elms and oaks, birches, wood of all sorts. For one who works with wood this may be a paradise. We shall see.

"In three rides I got all the way to the north side of Boston and by four o'clock I reached the house of Lance Bragdon.

"I must tell you this has been a disenchantment for me. We were such close friends in Italy! I do not think I deceive myself by thinking that, at that time, a genuine bond existed between us. I know that the places we went together and the things we did together assumed added significance, were experienced more deeply, because we were two close friends. I thought that this was something that would carry forward in time. I thought we could meet anywhere, anytime, and experience again the same mutual heightening of awareness. I have learned that friendship is no more durable than anything else in our lives. Not that Lance didn't ask me in and invite me for supper. It is just that whatever had been a basis for friendship before, was gone. I am trying to understand.

"This first night in Billerica - I found out that this is pronounced Bill Ricka - I am in a rooming house. The woman who owns and runs this establishment sits in her kitchen at the rear of the front hallway. She watches the front door from her vantage point. No one can come or go without her knowledge. At ten PM she locks the front door from the inside, she says. What happens if someone comes in later? I must find out. There are seven rooms for rent in this house and they are all occupied, now that I have taken the one next to the busier of the two bathrooms.

"Mrs. Connors is built like a cask. She wears a dress that is sleeveless and shapeless. Her bare arms look as if they could have lifted full barrels in the past, they are that sinewy. I don't think any roomers will try to take advantage of her.

"It is almost ten - the witching hour here, it seems. I am tired. I miss you. All three of you. *Buona notte Papà, Minca, Franca. Un abbraccione - Guido.*"

He would need envelopes and stamps in the morning. And things to eat, and to eat with, if he was to stay here.

He took off all his clothes except his undershorts and got into bed. It was warm in the room, almost too warm. An inch-wide bar of light from the hall came under the door. More light entered around the curtains at the window. If that bothered him he might see what could be done about it the next day.

He closed his eyes and heard a radio playing softly somewhere. It was not annoying. Someone with a heavy step came down the stairs and went into the bathroom. Weren't they supposed to use the bath on the third floor? Maybe it was already in use. When the toilets flushed, the rush of water in the pipes seemed to pass under the floor of his room. Perhaps it did. The house, with its eight different occupants, shifted and sighed, doors opened and closed, a chair was pushed back. Someone rolled over in a bed. Outside, a car passed in the street and there was the sound of wind in the big elm beyond the curtains.

Without the pack on his back, walking was a pleasure once more.

Guido had wakened at first light, was in and out of the bathroom before anyone else, and had found Mrs. Connors releasing the bolt on the front door. As a gesture of welcome, not to be repeated he was clearly made to understand, she gave him coffee and muffins in her kitchen and put her practiced eye to the appraisal of his capabilities.

"Work it is yer needin'?" she repeated when he asked. "Willin' an' able is all it takes. Ye'll find work aplenty. Try the markets, the shopping centers, anywhere you see construction. Yard work. Delivery work. There's no lack o' work."

She told him in which direction to head. "God bless ye, Lad," she said, half to herself as he set off. She'd seen the gold cross hanging from his neck.

The morning was chill. A few degrees colder and there would have been frost on the grass. But the sun was up and the day would be fair and warm. A magnolia on a front lawn had blossomed, thick waxy petals tinged with pink. Atop a low shrub a bird was singing, a small brownish streaky fellow with a spot in the center of the breast. He threw his head back and sang as if all the world belonged to him.

Something about the April morning, clean and fresh and full of promise, got inside Guido. He could still hear the sparrow singing even blocks beyond where he had left it, and the smell of the earth warming in the sun stayed in his lungs and his blood all through the day.

Before long, he came to an enormous black parking lot. Shops lined one edge of it. Only a couple of cars were parked there. It was early. Guido crossed the lot and looked through plate glass windows at quantities of goods so abundant he was confounded. Yet there was no one in sight. He heard voices, though. They came from the rear. He circled the buildings and discovered a trailer truck, backed up to an open door. Two men were shouting obscenities at each other - something about a sale that would begin in only two more hours and delivery that should have been yesterday afternoon. Who in Hell was going to get all this stuff into the store?

"Excuse me, please," Guido said to the man who was doing most of the yelling. "I am looking for work. Can you use me?"

Both men stopped swearing and stared at Guido. Then they looked at each other. One was wearing a business suit. He turned back to Guido. "You don't look very strong to me, Kid," he said. "You a good worker?"

"Try me," Guido said. "I will not disappoint you."

There was a hydraulic lift on the back of the trailer. The truck driver loaded a two-wheeler which was already in the truck and then lowered the platform.

"Follow me with that," the man in the suit said.

Guido tipped the load to find the point of balance and pushed it along to where the man said to stop. He learned how to slide the steel lip back from the six cartons of canned goods.

The man had taken off his jacket. "Now go back and get another load," he said. "I'll stack this for the sale. All you gotta do is keep ahead of me. Can you do it?"

"There is no worry," Guido said.

Another loaded dolly awaited him when he got the empty one back to the truck.

For two hours he went back and forth. The load was always the same but near the end it seemed to have doubled in weight. Once, he almost tipped it over crossing the sill to the store. For the last fifteen minutes a wrestler type, about the same age as Guido, appeared and took over for the man who turned out to be the store manager.

When Guido made the last trip it was a quarter to nine. The manager came out of a washroom putting on a clean shirt and tie.

"You saved the day, Kid," he said. "What's your name?"

Guido told him.

"Okay," the man said. "Look. This is for this morning." He gave Guido a ten dollar bill. "Now go into that office there, and wash up. Take a load off your feet. Wait till I get free and we'll talk about a job."

But when Mr. Tosnik learned that Guido had no social security number and was in the country on a tourist visa, he wasn't able to offer a regular job. "I can pay you out of petty cash for a week maybe, but it's illegal. You won't have any insurance coverage, no deductions, no health benefits. The company might be liable if you should get hurt. If you want to come around each morning half an hour before we open, I'll give you work for the day and at least a dollar an hour for the time you put in, but it's only a stopgap while you look for something else."

Guido thanked him. He worked there for exactly a week and saved a little money.

Walking back to his rooming house in the evening one day, he passed a house where an old man was getting ready to plant a vegetable garden. He stopped to watch.

"You know anything about raisin' vegetables, Young Feller?" the old man asked.

"We raised all our own vegetables in Italy," Guido said.

"Eyetalian eh? When I lived in Jersey every Eyetalian in the neighborhood had a garden. They could grow tomatoes in a tin can would beat anything you could buy."

"Squash and peppers, too, I bet," said Guido smiling.

"You got the secret, Boy? I do pretty good here. Used to, anyhow. But I was never even in competition down in Jersey."

"I could help you. I need work. Can you pay a dollar an hour?"

"Where you stayin' now?"

"Just down the street. With Mrs. Connors."

"I know the woman. Strong as a horse and just about as pretty. Probably chargin' you all outdoors for some itty-bitty room. Suppose I give you a real room in my house and three meals a day, all you can eat, while you get my garden in and clean up the yard. How's that sound?"

"I'd need a little cash too."

"Hmmm. Five dollars a day, mebbe?"

Guido put out his hand. "Is a deal," he said.

The old man grinned and they shook on it and the next morning Guido moved into a spacious immaculate room at the rear of Mr. Spinner's house. They ate together in a kitchen that gleamed from ceiling to rubber-tiled floor.

"Lived alone for eighteen years now," Mr. Spinner said. "Miss havin' someone to talk to but I like havin' everything just so."

He had an ancient Ford truck. The two of them drove to a local dairy farm and got three loads of cow manure that had aged about six months. It was free. Guido did all the heavy work. At seventy-four, Mr. Spinner was no longer able to do much more than drive and cook and keep his pots shining. He sure could talk, too.

Guido found it easy to get along with the old man. He enjoyed spreading the manure and turning it under while Spinner stood by gabbing and advising.

At the rear of the property was a tool shed. One side of it faced south and had sun on it almost all day. Guido built a cold frame there, using some old storm windows as covers. He started winter squash and pumpkins in it, and broccoli and flats of tomatoes to be transplanted later when there wouldn't be any more chance of frost.

At the dump, where they went in the truck, he spotted a rug someone had thrown out and they brought it back to spread over the cold frame when the nights were likely to get especially cold.

Nearly three weeks passed before Guido completed all the jobs that needed doing around Mr. Spinner's home. The old man had grown attached to him by then, but he didn't have five dollars a day to give away for no value received. "Wisht I could," he said, "but I guess I gotta turn you loose."

Once a month he drove down to Boston to go shopping. He took Guido along and turned him loose. "Don't know what you'll find to do here," he said, when they parted, "but this is the city and it's got a lot more opportunities than a two-bit town like Billerica. You'll make out. I do thank you for your help. Mebbe you'll drop me a line from time to time."

They had parked on Boylston Street. Guido crossed to the Common and strolled toward the capitol dome which he saw shining ahead of him. There were children on tricycles on the walks and old folks on the benches. The big trees were coming into leaf.

He had not seen Lance again after the first night in Billerica. Lance hadn't come to find him and he hadn't wanted to go to his friend's house again. Friend? One-time friend. Friend no longer. What was it about friendship? Was some mutual activity essential? Was that what created the bond? And when you were no longer both involved in studying together in school, or in being together in military service, or in working together at the same job, then the thing you had called friendship dissolved - was that it?

But his father still talked about a friend from his childhood who had moved to Torino. They hadn't seen each other for many years, yet they still kept in touch. At least they exchanged cards at Easter. Was that friendship? If they were to meet again, what relationship would emerge?

Maybe what had happened with Lance was that Lance had led Guido to expect too much of him. He had been the big-shot American who was going to succeed, who couldn't lose, and when Guido had appeared, Lance had realized how shabby, how *meschino*, his life had become. It had shamed him. And since he hadn't been able to make anything of himself yet (and probably never would) there was no way he could do anything for Guido - a further cause for remorse, in view of the wild promises of help he had made only two years before.

From the State House, Guido turned down Beacon Street and was surprised to see a sign proclaiming Joy Street. Did the august members of the General Court maintain whorehouses in the shadow of the golden cupola? He walked up Joy Street but didn't see any shuttered windows. Nothing looked suspicious to him. But of course he didn't know what to look for.

Pinckney Street led him downhill to Louisburg Square. The neatly tended, bow-fronted brick buildings around the central park of shrubbery and trees delighted his eyes. There were cobblestones underfoot, not the flat *dalle* of so many Tuscan streets, but knobbly irregular stones that made for difficult walking. On one corner, a giant vine of wisteria grew up the side of a house. It would be blooming before much longer. The memory of that same vine, *il glicine*, on stone walls in the country at home made him stop and wonder what he was doing here, alone, in this land he did not understand. Was he mad to have come? Was there a future here for him? If so, would it be a better one than he could have had in the land of his birth? But the moment of doubt passed. He thought how easily he had been able to get from one place to another and how quickly he had found work that covered his needs. Surely there was a place for him in America.

On Myrtle Street, he saw a sign in a window that said ROOM. The solidly paneled wooden door to the house had four pieces of glass at its top. They had the thick wavy look of the bottoms of bottles. A brass knocker in the center of the door seemed to be the only means of announcing one's presence. Guido lifted it and let it fall twice and then waited.

Eventually the door opened on a man wearing slippers and chino pants and a sweater that was unraveling at cuff and neck and elbow. He was between forty-five and sixty years old, stooped. His teeth were crooked and yellow.

"You have a room for rent?" Guido asked.

The man squinted. He looked as if he might just close the door without answering. Then he asked. "You a student?"

Guido didn't know what sort of query this was. Was there a right answer? Should he say Yes? Was that a sign of class, to be a student? But a student of what? "No," he said, at last. "I am a workman."

The sour expression on the man's face didn't change. "You can't bring any women in this house," he said.

Guido was tempted to say that he didn't even know any women in this country, but he said: "I understand."

"What kind of work you do?"

"I am a woodworker."

Slowly the man nodded. "I'll show you the room," he said. He led the way up two flights of beautifully constructed curving stairs. The room was one of two at the rear on the third floor. It had a fireplace that was plastered shut and the partition separating it from the other rear room had obviously been put in by someone in a hurry to make one room into two. A cot, a table, a wooden chair, a bureau and a standing lamp made up the furniture. The one window looked out on a small courtyard. A bathroom, across the hall, served all four rooms on that floor.

"Six dollars a week," the man said. "No hot plates. No visitors. Wednesday, if you bring me a sheet, pillowcase and towel, I give you a clean one in exchange. You take care of your own room.

Dry mop's on the landing."

The bed was made and the room was clean. A blue towel hung on the back of the chair.

The old geezer was eyeing Guido again. "This is a place to sleep. Nothing else. You want it?"

"I'll take it," Guido said.

He paid the six dollars and got a key to the front door and to his room. He spelled out his name for the owner, Mr. Anderson, who wrote it in a spiral notebook and then disappeared into his own quarters on the ground floor.

The house was silent that mid-afternoon. Guido put the contents of his backpack in the drawers of the bureau and opened the window. It had turned warm, warmer out than in, where the night's chill still lingered. There was a filtering of soot on the window sill, but the air that entered had an earth smell. The courtyard of the house he was in was one of many below him. Brick walls surrounded patios - some tended, with flagstones and flower beds, some little more than junk heaps, with rotting boards and wooden cases stacked in them. A walkway snaked its way from a nearby building between walls nine feet high to a point out of sight in the direction of Pinckney Street.

He heard muffled voices and traffic sounds from outside, but in his own house there could have been no one at that hour, or perhaps anyone there was asleep.

Later, roomers came in. He could hear the front door slam each time, then the sounds of steps on the stairs, a trip to the bathroom, doors to rooms closing - some gently, others with a whack. There was a lot of coming and going from five to seven. Then it grew quieter. Several radios played, but more or less cancelled each other out.

You were not supposed to prepare any food in your room, the owner had said, but odors of many sorts reached Guido. He found out, in time, there were all kinds of take-out orders you could pick up on the way home - pizza, fried chicken, chowder, hamburg and onions, something called submarine sandwiches.

All Mr. Anderson's tenants were working people. He wouldn't let a student into his house. They were always wise guys, he said, and they raised Cain and stayed up all night. He liked people who worked regular jobs and had to get to bed early in order to leave early in the morning.

A woman had the large front room on the second floor. Sometimes she left her door open. She had lived in that same room for over a decade and the odors of all those years of perspiring female occupancy seemed to have accumulated there without opportunity to dissipate. Miss Zorna was fat and flabby. She worked in a hardware store keeping the accounts. Her smile was round, open-mouthed, and she spoke in a phlegmy contralto which might have been seductive, but the lugubrious effluvium which clung to her, a mixture of deodorants and heavy perfume and stale bedclothes, drove away all but stray dogs in the street.

A parking lot attendant had the room next to Guido. Pakradoonian was his name, a short tough dark man who told Guido his salary was sixty a week, but he doubled it with the tips he collected and then he made another hundred a week running numbers. Where did it all go? Week-ends he went to the track. Someday, wait and see, he was going to hit a "long shot" and then... what? Guido realized he shouldn't have asked. It was the dream of the long shot that kept Pakradoonian going, that kept him alive. If it ever became a reality he would have to spend the money quickly in order to start over.

Saturdays and Sundays, holidays too, the rooming house changed character. Some of the roomers seemed to spend all forty-eight hours sleeping. Others, went away to visit relatives - ex-wives, parents, children.

Two men on the top floor, both in their fifties, always spent the time drinking. They weren't boistrous. They didn't fight. They drank, and talked to each other about themselves - telling their lives over in versions they had come to believe were the true ones. Twice, Guido listened to them from the hallway, the slurred voices recounting misadventure and misfortune, repetitious, monotonous, an antiphony of commiseration, a binding reciprocal cementing of kinship.

Guido walked daily in the city. Boston felt good to him. In no time he knew every corner of Beacon Hill, from the dilapidated alleyway behind Temple Street to the restrained elegance of Mt. Vernon and West Cedar. He loved the variety of the shops along Charles and the mingling there of blue-blooded dowagers and panhandlers, transvestite and pugilist. In the antique shops, he saw many things that had come from Italy and he smiled, noticing how much of what was supposed to be authentic had been more or less artfully restored or recreated. There would be work for him. No hurry.

In the West End, one day, a man over six feet tall and wide as a doorway came rocking toward him. He wore a gray suit with torn cuffs and holes everywhere. Over it was a World War I greatcoat that came to his ankles and could have seen service as a horse blanket - perhaps it had.

The man stopped in front of Guido, blocking his way, and spread his arms.

"You have come from afar," he said, fiercely staring into Guido's eyes.

"You are the son of an honorable man but you will find no joy in paternity yourself. A light shines from you. You are among the chosen."

Was he looking for a handout? Guido was unsure. He was a little apprehensive too. There was madness in the fellow and he was a giant.

"I will tell you a story."

Guido noticed a man passing on the other side of the street.

Their eyes met. The passerby pointed to the man in the greatcoat, then tapped his temple with a forefinger.

"There was once a young man from Petrovskoye. Strong as a lion. Swift. Many-talented. He left his home - the people he loved and the people who loved him. He crossed mountains and deserts and oceans. Through war and through pestilence he voyaged to come to the land called America, to find greatness and wealth. And he found here only that from which he fled."

"You are telling me your story," Guido said. "It is not a happy one."

The long arms in the olive-drab horse blanket rose again, spread wide and hung there a moment. Then hands strong enough to twist iron fell to Guido's shoulders, touching him gently.

"You have never seen me before and you know that?"

"You have never seen me before," Guido answered, "but you guessed that I had come from afar."

There was an odor of old mortar and plaster mingled with urine coming from the man. Guido wanted to step back but was unable to do so.

"I have a gift of seeing what is the truth for others," said the giant. "My own truth I cannot see."

The accent was heavy. It had to be Russian, but overlain with a curious Biblical turn of phrase. Guido felt a surge of affection for the man. They were both foreigners in an alien land. For this other one, though, there had been no profit in coming.

"We are all foreigners here," the man said, as if reading Guido's thought. "Russian Jews, like me, Sicilians, Poles, Greeks. You can walk through the neighborhoods of the city of Boston and find enclaves of every nationality on earth, from the Orient, to Africa, to South America. This is a thing of wonder. A thing of beauty. A cause of heartbreak. You will see, Young Man."

And with that he strode away, muttering, the coat swaying.

Guido ran into a mailman, the same day, who knew the

Russian.

"He's crazy, the mailman said. "They've put him away a dozen times. He's a pest. He stops traffic and spouts nutty stuff like how the world is about to end unless we all show love for each other instead of hatred. Can you imagine loving him? He sleeps in abandoned buildings or the subway. He scavenges in trash cans. They say he steals. When he gets angry, he's dangerous. He threw a detective clean through a plate glass window a couple of years ago because the guy called him a bum and a Kike. Don't go getting friendly with him. You'll regret it."

But Guido could not believe it. He had seen the loneliness in the man and sensed that this was something shared by thousands of others who lived in the city, no doubt by people everywhere in the world. But to be mad, besides, not totally insane, just half over the line, would make you an outcast, one to be avoided, so that would push you further toward a place where all human intercourse might end. Just the loneliness could drive you mad, and the madness would build a wall around you.

- How will I deal with this? Guido asked himself. Already I lie down at night and with the light out I feel the emptiness spreading outward around me. I am alone here. There is no one who would even notice if I dropped through a hole in the sidewalk and disappeared forever.

He had walked out of the West End and was in a place full of pushcarts and fruit stands, small shops, trucks being loaded and unloaded, and in a Babel of tongues he was hearing words in Italian, whole phrases. Where was he? These were not the voices of Tuscany. They were southern voices.

"*Ma scusi,*" Guido said to a man who stood by a cart laden with asparagus and rhubarb. "*Lei viene dall'Italia?*"

Was the man from Italy? He gave Guido a look that conveyed only contempt. "*E voi. Venite dall'Etiopia?*...And you. You come from Ethiopia?"

Guido turned away. He was surrounded by Italians and they were more foreign to him than the college types and Irish matrons here doing their shopping. Did he come from Ethiopia? What an answer to a civil query! But his had been a stupid question. Of course the man came from Italy. The hat with the brim drooping on all sides, the heavy black mustache, the sloping shoulders in the stained brown jacket, the bulging paunch, the flat-footed stance - and the pushcart that might have come with him right off the streets of Naples - what else could he be? Where else could he have come from if not Italy?

So the undisguised sneer in his voice when he answered, was it for the one who asked a dumb question, or for the one who had forsaken his homeland yet changed nothing in his life?

Guido bought three oranges. He found a place where there was fresh-baked Italian-looking bread and a cheese shop that sold him a quarter pound of *gorgonzola*.

In a square commemorating Paul Revere, he sat on a bench and ate his lunch. The bread, still warm, did not have the weight and substance of true country bread, but it was the closest thing to it he had tasted since leaving home. The *gorgonzola* was not as ripe as it should have been, but it was good. So were the oranges.

He ate with pleasure, taking his time, cutting the bread with the long-bladed pocket knife he always carried, and spreading the slightly crumbly cheese on it, peeling each orange slowly and savoring the juices.

A man with an ebony cane, wearing a hat with a bright orange feather in it, his suit carefully tailored and his black shoes gleaming, sat next to Guido on the bench.

"*Buon appetito*," he said.

"*Altretanto a Lei*...Same to you," Guido replied, seeing that the man was unwrapping something that looked like a meat pie.

"I haven't seen you here before," the man said. His voice was deep, the accent heavy.

"This is the first time I am come to this part of town," Guido said.

"And what do you think of this part of town?"

"*Mi piace molto*...I like it a lot," Guido said, hoping the man would reply in Italian as he had begun.

But this didn't happen. When the man spoke again he reverted to English. "Many come to wander in the North End," he said.

There was a note of warning in the statement. Was the man saying that this territory was already staked out? Walk here, but tread lightly? Was Guido sitting in someone else's place?

This old man, surely in his seventies or eighties, had a proprietary air. Maybe he came each day at this hour to sit on the east end of this same bench and eat his beef pie.

"Would you care for a section of my orange?" Guido asked.

The old man turned then. He had to rotate his whole body, shifting thin buttocks on the bench in order to face Guido. Spare flesh over his large jawbone and jutting cheekbones was firm and taut. His brow was a looming cliff above deep eye sockets. "Thank you," he said, extending an arthritic, joint-crippled talon to accept the proffered section of orange.

Guido, in that moment, lost all sense of where he was and the time in which he was living. Under the scrutiny of this gaunt eagle he had become a petitioner before a *seigneur*, his offer of a piece of fruit symbolic, an ancient ritual repeated.

The old man, too, seemed aware of this. Here, in America, in the twentieth century, two Italians who had never met before, whose backgrounds were widely divergent, separated in years by five decades or more, had yet reenacted a rite from the Middle Ages.

"Thank you," the old man said again, and the moment was over. Perhaps it had not even existed.

"How long have you been in America?"

"Only a couple of weeks," Guido said.

"Did you come here to study?"

"No. I came because I had a friend, an American I met at the end of the war."

"You found this friend?"

"I did."

"There is some hesitation in your voice."

Guido had finished eating. His fingers were sticky. He had put the orange peelings inside the paper bag they'd come in, along with the wax paper that had been around the cheese.

"It is true," he said. "I found the person who had been my friend, but the circumstances which made us friends in Italy did not exist here."

"You have had a deception."

"It has been a disappointment. I might never have decided to come here if I had not met Lance Bragdon. Maybe I shouldn't have come." He twisted the paper bag tight and looked for somewhere to dispose of it.

"Do you have a trade?" the old man asked.

"*Sono falegname*."

"A carpenter. A woodworker. Excellent. If you are an accomplished artisan you will have no trouble finding work. Here, everything is mass-produced. Machines can do almost anything. But only the human hand can produce a work of art. The old crafts are vanishing, but they are much in demand."

Twice, as they talked, someone had passed and bowed. "Don Tito," they said, and their words were acknowledged by a two-fingered salute.

"I am known here as Don Tito di Montefalcone," the old man said, introducing himself. "And you?"

"Guido Bussatti, from Castiglion Fiorentino, near Arezzo."

"Aha!" Don Tito had raised one eyebrow. "So you are one of the famous *maledetti Toscani*."

"I don't think anyone calls us 'accursed Tuscans' anymore,"

Guido said.

"You are right. Still, of the many Italians who are here in America, very few share your origins. Those from central Italy are mostly intellectuals at the universities, or they are in business - importing, exporting. They tend not to associate with the rest of us."

Guido could not help thinking of his uncle Attilio. This applied to him. Attilio had not even wanted to remain long in contact with his own nephew, and surely he would never have considered sitting on a park bench, like a common laborer, eating cheese and bread and sharing an orange with an aged Sicilian.

Don Tito had a small shop nearby, Guido discovered a few days later. It was not clear what his business was. People came to the shop, men mostly. They addressed Don Tito with respect. Sometimes they sat and chatted for a while. Much of the talk was in English, but a phrase now and then in an inscrutable Sicilian dialect, an oath, an admonition, lent an air of conspiracy to conversations that were elliptical, or seemed to have little point.

Guido found work, thanks to Don Tito, in a store in the North End where new garish borax furniture was sold. It did a brisk business in repairs. The shop was well equipped. A man named Tonino took care of re-glueing and patching things of no particular worth. Guido was given the better items which needed refinishing or reconstruction and immediately became an indispensible member of the firm.

Since he was only a block away, when there were slack times he often dropped in on Don Tito who had somehow become his benefactor.

A Wednesday afternoon in May the two were together when a young woman entered. She was only a silhouette against the light at the doorway. Then she stepped in and Guido saw she was slender and well formed, graceful. She had black wavy hair cut short and parted on the right so that from the left her face was largely hidden. But from the right her good strong features were easily seen.

"Gimme twenty, Grumps," she said, extending her hand.

"And what do you need so much for, may I ask?"

"Ma says to buy steak for your supper. You're coming tonight. And she wants *ravioli* for starters and *mille foglie* for dessert. I'll be lucky if twenty's enough."

"You know I can't eat so many rich things."

"I know you always say it and then you eat as much as anyone."

Don Tito, grumbling, opened a small metal box that sat on the table in front of him. It was packed with bills. He peeled off a twenty and handed it to the girl.

"See you tonight," she said, and was gone.

"That one!" Don Tito said. "She's wild. Eighteen this week. She's the youngest of my three granddaughters. Every time I see her she has some new notion. Last week she was going to be an airline hostess. Before that, to study acting. Another day, go visit my brother in Buenos Aires. She needs something to settle her down. A husband and a couple of kids. That would teach her about real life."

Guido was only half listening. Don Tito noticed.

"So. She caught your eye, my young friend. I'm not surprised. There is fire in that child and the way she moves, no man could sit still or turn away. *M'attenzione. Piano, piano.* She is family and we cling to the old ways here."

The patriarch was speaking, not the kindly benefactor. Guido heard the difference. He would not forget.

Women had filled only a small part of his life until then. In the army he had gone with companions to *case chiuse*...closed houses, in the towns where they were stationed. Those experiences had left him more restless than gratified. He hadn't minded paying. It relieved some of the insistent preoccupation with sex which seemed never to leave him, but to pay, and to use a stranger, and then to be hustled out after ten minutes without even taking off your shoes, was not much better than the pleasure you could give yourself, and that with no risk of disease.

In his own village, he had flirted with the girls he knew and had thought for a while he was in love with one who was plump and comely, who looked at him with wide slightly frightened eyes and never spoke. But he had learned nothing about love and knew that his ignorance was nearly total.

Now, in the space of only a few moments, he sensed that his expectations in life had been altered. He wanted to follow this young woman and stop her and speak to her. He imagined himself touching her shoulder and saying...saying what? How would he gain her attention? Suppose she took one look at him and that was enough? Suppose she saw nothing in him?

"May I ask you, Don Tito, what is the name of your granddaughter?"

Don Tito shifted his leathery behind on the chair so he could look straight at Guido. "You may ask, Guido Bussatti. My granddaughter's name is Luciana Cardullo. Her father, my son-in-law, owns a trucking company. He is a man of few words, most of which are obscenitites. One does not trifle with him. Or with anyone in his family. Do you understand?"

It was as if they were back on the bench that first time they met when Don Tito said: "Many come to wander in the North End." To walk here circumspectly was one thing; to pause was another.

"I understand, Don Tito. I will respect your wishes and any counsel you choose to give me. Now I must return to work."

A week passed. In his mind, Guido saw Luciana meeting him where he worked or coming toward him in the street. He tried to guess what they might say to one another. He remembered her voice when she spoke to her grandfather. It was pitched low for a woman. Was there a coarseness in it, or was that an earthy sensuality he heard?

- Stop dreaming, he told himself. You will re-make her and when you see her again she will not measure up to the dream. But he could not stop thinking about her. Was it just because he was far from home, he wondered? Was it just being lonely that made the first pretty girl her saw seem special? He tried to be rational about it. The streets were full of young women. He stared at them. Some of them stared back. A few even smiled. But they could not be compared with Luciana. He had to see her again. It was a necessity.

When he did meet her again she was coming out of a fish store with a package in her hands. She was frowning. He stopped before her. "You seem to be troubled, Luciana," he said.

She looked up at him, the frown still on her face, ready to tell him to mind his own business. Then she remembered him. "Oh. You're the one Grumps keeps talking about. Guido. Yes?"

"That's right. I hope you have heard good things from your grandfather."

She tossed some of the dark hair away from her face. "Well, let me see," she said. "He says that you are very shy, that you need a haircut, that sometimes you seem like a lost child."

She was teasing him. It was not likely that Don Tito had spoken that way about him. But he had spoken. To Luciana. That was good.

"Would it be too bold and out of character if I offered to carry this package you were looking at with so much distaste?"

She thrust it at him and he took it.

"It is *baccalà*," said said. "For Grumps. He'd rather eat that smelly old fish than have a good roast." She put her palms to her nose. "My hands stink already. Yours will too."

"I'm surprised you don't carry *una rete* for shopping. How do you call that in English?"

"I don't know what...Oh, I bet it means a net bag. Good idea.

I'll buy one right now. Come on."

She took him in tow and he was glad to follow her as she shopped. She found a net shopping bag and the fish package went into it. She bought bread and fruit and lettuce and parsley. At the butcher's she made them cut the meat to her specifications and then took a dollar off the price they wanted to charge her. There were protests but she ignored them.

Guido walked her to the door of her building. "Now that I know where you live, may I come to call on you some evening?" he asked.

She tipped her head in order to have both eyes on him. Her gaze was intense. "You're not too shy after all, are you? Let me see. I'm very busy, you know. How about tonight?"

Guido laughed. "That will be fine. Eight o'clock?"

"Sure. And you'll meet my family. Third floor. Eight. See you."

For the rest of the day, Guido was as one bemused. He did his work but had no recollection of doing it. He finished. He went back to Myrtle Street. He ate what he brought home with him. It was only six o'clock. When the bathroom was free he went in and showered and shaved. He had never shaved twice in the same day before. He noticed that the big bush of almost kinky black hair on his head did need cutting. Fresh-washed it stood higher than ever.

- I look as if I came out of Africa, he thought. At least my skin is not too dark.

He put on a new white shirt and a pair of clean pants. He shined his only pair of good shoes. A tie? He didn't like to wear one. Would he seem too casual without it? He put one on, but a minute later took it off and placed it back in the drawer. It was still only six-thirty. An endless hour later he left the house and started walking. He knew he'd be early but he couldn't just sit on the edge of his bed forever.

A woman his own height answered his knock. She opened the door all the way and stood there an instant looking at him. She was straight and a little stiff, it seemed, with her head held back. Her dark dress had a thin belt drawn tight above good hips, under a generous bust. She smiled.

"*Signora Cardullo?*" Guido asked.

"And you must be Guido Bussatti," she said. "Come in. Come in. Luciana is not yet ready. We'll sit in the kitchen. Once we had a living room, but Paolino took it for his room. Now we live all in the kitchen."

This last-named room was enormous and had everything - a two-door refrigerator/freezer, a double sink of stainless steel, a spotless gas range, peach-colored countertops, cabinets with brass handles along an entire wall. An oblong wooden table made of walnut filled the center of the room. Five chairs surrounded it and there was room for several more. A radio blocked a window. The heavy-duty linoleum on the floor matched the counter tops and had been installed by professionals. A realistic Sacred Heart hung in a frame between the radio and a gaudy calendar.

At the table, in his undershirt, sat a man of forty. He was completely bald, yet his arms, all the way to the wrists, were covered with a mat of black hair. Hair grew on the tops of his shoulders and a thick pelt was visible on his back and over his chest. He had the build of one of those phony wrestlers who were coming into vogue, but he did not look like one who would engage in any phony contest. It would be for real - had been, by the look of the scars on his arms and his face.

He put down the paper he had been reading, as Guido entered, and got to his feet. He was not tall. His legs were short and bowed. He was all torso. Someday it would go fatty and soft, but for now it was a kind of vulcanized layering of tendons and muscle.

"Francesco Cardullo," he said, extending his hand.

Guido introduced himself and put his own hand in that of the other. There was no attempt to show off the strength that was there.

"Siddown," Cardullo ordered. "Mamma, you got some coffee maybe?"

Mrs. Cardullo brought cups and saucers to the table, along with a pot of coffee that was ready. She produced cream and sugar, too, and a plate full of pastry. She did not sit at the table but stood a little to the rear of Guido.

"So yer workin' down to Panaschi's."

Guido had not been prepared for this sort of test. He was nervous. Cardullo sat opposite him like some wartime commander before a new recruit. He would have intimidated a whole room full of conscripts. It was not hard to immagine him giving orders to have an enemy brought before him for interrogation, or, subsequently, to be executed at dawn.

"Yes," Guido said. "I'm in the back room there. Tonino does most of the work. He's very quick. Lots of the new furniture is *robaccia*, not good stuff. It breaks easily and has to be repaired. Tonino handles that part. They give me the work that takes greater care."

The heavy bald head nodded slightly. "Don Tito says you have already a solid reputation as a workman."

"Don Tito is kind to say it. He has been good to me."

A young man, not long out of high school, came into the room.

"This is Paolino," Cardullo said, "my son that works with me. Marcello, my other son, was too fancy for driving trucks. He sits now behind a desk at a finance business."

Guido thought he could hear a sigh from Mrs. Cardullo, but she was behind him and he couldn't turn to look at her.

"Where you goin' tonight?" Cardullo asked his son.

"Just down to the corner, Pop."

"An' what's on the corner so important?"

"Nothin', Pop. My friends are there. We get together."

"You be home early. Don't forget it."

He was free to go and he scooted.

"Young guys today," Cardullo muttered. "Everyone's gotta car. You never know what they gonna do."

A door opened and closed somewhere deeper in the apartment and Guido heard footsteps approaching. Luciana entered the kitchen as Guido got to his feet.

Time stopped. He looked at her and could not have told where he was or how he got there.

She had heels on. She wore a light beige dress that just touched her knees. Against the black of her hair, her skin was magnolia blossom white, and at the low neckline of her dress, behind a ruffle, her rambunctious breasts rippled and quivered.

"Hi," she said.

"Such an entrance," her mother said. "Like an actress she comes."

"That's my baby." It was Cardullo speaking. "An' I don't want no foolin' around. Siddown again." He was addressing Guido. "Tell me, Guido Bussatti. Do you have serious intentions?"

"Pop," Luciana said. "What are you talking about?"

"You know what I'm talkin' about. Well?" insisted the father.

"Mr. Cardullo," Guido began, trying to collect his wits, off balance from this belligerent preemptive advance on territory where no claims had been formulated or even conceived, "I believe that you will find I am a serious person."

"How much money you make now?"

"Pop!" Luciana protested. "Guido and I only met for one minute at Don Tito's a week ago. Today we shopped for the roast for ten minutes. Slow down. Hold your horses!"

"Hold my horses! Is that a way for a child to speak to her father? I'll tell you something. It's <u>your</u> horses galloping away into the woods that have me worried."

Luciana's eyes were wide and round. She put her fists on her hips. "And where are the woods in the North End? Where are they in this kitchen for that matter? If I find them I'll gallop into them just to thank you for pointing them out."

Cardullo started to get to his feet. His face and all his bald head were flushed to cranberry red.

"*Signor Cardullo*," Guido said. "*Un momento*. You asked me a question. I don't mind answering. I understand your concern. To have a daughter like yours must be a heavy responsibility. What do I earn? Fifty-seven dollars a week now. But that will improve. Is that what you wanted to know?"

Cardullo settled back into his chair. His wife and daughter were staring at Guido. "You are a reasonable man, Guido Bussatti, and I am too often hot-headed. I will expect you to be as honorable as you are reasonable. I will count on you." He shot a distrustful look at Luciana. "Enough said." With that he disappeared behind his newspaper.

Luciana went around the table and kissed her father's gleaming pate. "We'll walk up Snow Hill Street and be back within an hour," she said.

Her father grunted. Her mother came with them to the hall. "Be sure to be back in less than an hour," she whispered.

They escaped down the stairs and stepped out into the warm June night. Luciana took Guido's hand. Just the touch of her fingers made him catch his breath.

The street was full of people. It was early. As they walked up the hill more and more lights remained behind them, and when they looked out over the river toward Charlestown they could even distinguish a few stars through the impure air above the city.

By the cemetery they stopped. Was anyone watching them. They stood facing each other and both knew what would happen. Guido put his hands on Luciana's waist and drew her against him. Her arms went over his and around his neck, her hands dancing on his hair and his ears, then cupping his cheeks.

The fullness and warmth of her the length of his body filled him with desire such as he had never known before. Not only was there the overwhelming physical need, embarrassingly apparent to her too, but tenderness, like a rising tide, overflowed in him and he knew he wanted to hold this woman for the rest of his life, to provide for her and protect her and to be the one to whom she turned.

"Luciana..." he started to say. But she put a finger against his lips, then took it away and raised her mouth to his.

There was a taste of blackberries on her upper lip from the pastry she had eaten, and a hot faint flavor of walnut, perhaps, on the tongue she let him caress with his own. The eagerness she showed him, the passion in her, made him dizzy.

No telling how long they might have clung to each other had a car not rounded the corner, headlights swinging in a long arc. They broke apart and walked to where the playground was below them, the small park behind them. A boat whistle sounded, the roar of a plane taking off from Logan, traffic's mutter - city sounds mingling with voices and music from a radio in a window somewhere.

Much later, back in his room on Beacon Hill, Guido relived the evening again and again. He could not believe this had happened to him in such an immediate, total way. Perhaps he was simply overcome with a physical attraction which begged for consummation. What, after all, was Luciana except a desirable woman, like so many others? What special qualities did she possess? But when he sought answers to these questions the memory of the taste of her mouth came between him and any rational thought. He could feel her body against his. Even the perfume she wore was still on the hand she had held. He moved his palm in front of his face and inhaled and she was almost palpably with him again.

- Is it possible, he asked himself, that certain people are right for each other, nothing more complicated than that? If two are about the same age and see no glaring faults in each other and if circumstances are not adverse, is it enough that one should be male and the other female? He had expected love to be more subtle, to involve many elements. Was he blind then? Is love blind?

But she was beautiful. *Benedett'Iddio*, how radiantly beautiful she was. A man would be blind indeed not to see that. Don Tito had said it too, and he was old enough to know. This was a serious matter.

For two days he had no chance to get away from his job. On the third afternoon he took an hour and went to see the old man.

Two very rough-looking characters were in the shop when Guido arrived. They glared at Guido, nodded to Don Tito, and left.

"So, Guido Bussatti, you have remembered that I am here."

"I wanted to come to see you sooner, Don Tito, but there was much work."

"And what was on your mind?"

"I need to talk with you."

"Yes?"

"It is..." On the point of speaking, Guido found himself at a loss to put into words what he had come to ask. Had he even come to ask something?"

"It is about my granddaughter, isn't it?"

"Yes."

"You saw her the other evening. You met my son-in-law."

"I ran into Luciana when she was shopping and walked her to her home. That evening I went there to see her and I met her mother and father and a brother, Paolino I think was his name."

Don Tito stretched one of his arms and a joint cracked at the shoulder. "A boy who needs watching," he said. "And what did you think of Francesco Cardullo?"

Guido knew he was on the spot this time. "Don Tito," he said, "you told me he was a man of few words. He is truly one who comes straight to the point."

The old man was smiling. He knew about the scene in the kitchen then. "So you found that out," he said. "Now you know that he is not an easy man to deal with. But don't misunderstand. In his own way and by his own lights he has been a good father and a good husband. Devoted. A provider who has never failed to do for his family what was expected. He works as hard as any man I know."

Don Tito let his gaze shift away from Guido. He looked out the top of the window, through the fly-specked glass and the dust. He was speaking for Guido as much as for himself but it was a past long gone he was seeing. "Teresa, when she was young, was every bit as lovely as Luciana. She had the same fire in her and the same vivid contrast between her jet black hair and her flawless white skin. Francesco Cardullo saw her and came to me and told me - not, *con permesso, Don Tito* - he came and he told me: 'I am going to marry your daughter, Teresa.' I said I would consult with my daughter. He said that was as it should be, that if she did not want to have him, he would accept that, but nothing else was admissible.

"There were others who would have married her, several, for she was a beauty. He would have fought them. I think he would have killed them had they dared to compete with him. Teresa was young. She was in a fever to be married. Cardullo was, and still is, a powerful and determined man.

"She has not been unhappy with him. He has given her security, children. She exists as a shadow to him, it is true. Perhaps my wife, whom I value now as I should have when she was alive, existed also as a shadow to me - a servant, a handmaiden.

"But the old ways are changing, Guido Bussatti. It may, or may not, be for the better. Luciana will be nobody's shadow."

Don Tito looked back at Guido and paused. Then he asked: "Tell me, please, my young friend, are you strongly religious?"

"I am a Catholic, Don Tito."

"A 'good Catholic,' as they say? A fervent Catholic? A go-to-Mass-once-a-year-Catholic?"

"I have never questioned my faith," Guido said. "I guess religion is not a big part of my life."

Where was all this leading? Guido could not be sure. He wanted to be honest. At the same time, he didn't want to say anything wrong.

"All the women in my family," Don Tito said, "have been devout Catholics. Maybe religion is more for women than for men. A man controls his destiny. A woman does not. Or am I wrong, Guido Bussatti?"

"Are you telling me something, Don Tito?"

For the first time, Guido saw something in the old man's manner which was upsetting. There was uncertainty there. His lean frame and the hollows in his face where there had once been solid flesh, spoke of frailty.

"I am looking for answers, too," Don Tito said. "The world keeps changing. What we once accepted as truth, whether it was or not, we could live with. We could count on it. In the Catholic marriage ceremony the priest proclaims: 'And the wife shall follow the husband.' No one questioned this in the past. It was taken for granted. We made book on it, you might say. A sure thing.

"Today, when your generation marries, there is divorce - not in the eyes of the Church, of course. But the Church is no longer the power that it once was.

"Today there is contraception in many ways. There may be legal abortion someday now. I hear talk of trial marriage and wife-swapping. What is happening? I feel myself fossilized in a past that was safer, surer. Were the old ways all wrong? Were they all a lie? The ground trembles under my feet today. There is no more sure footing for me.

"I say all this to you because this changed world is the one in which you must live and survive. You are here this afternoon, I know, because you are in love. It is something one sees in your face. Also, Luciana has been here to see me. I told you, all the women in my family have been devout Catholics. They were. Luciana is not one of them. I don't know what she believes. She changes faster than the world around her. If religion is a foundation on which you expect to build, my friend, then your feelings for Luciana will need to be regarded closely."

An arrow of sunlight began to come through the window. It fell on the desk between Guido and Don Tito.

"I don't think that too little religion could bother me," Guido said. "Luciana should be free to believe whatever she wants. I would be troubled if she wanted to convert me to some other faith. Even that, though, would be more amusing than serious."

"You are a very easy-going person, Guido Bussatti. But if you should marry Luciana, for father-in-law you would have a man your exact opposite."

"I would not make my home with my father-in-law."

"Where would you live? What are your plans?"

Guido hadn't begun to think this far ahead. "I don't know," he said. "Those are questions for which I need to find answers. It seems I can make a living in this country without much difficulty. If I should marry I should be able to support a wife without any trouble. Maybe the question is: Should I be thinking of something so serious? Am I crazy to contemplate marriage to someone I've only seen for a couple of hours?"

"Is one any less crazy to contemplate marriage to someone known for years?"

"You think it's a gamble in any case, is that it?"

"In the old days many marriages were made without even consulting the parties involved. Were there more bad marriages then?"

"I wouldn't know about that," Guido said. "But is it enough,

Don Tito, to want someone so much that it hurts?"

"What do you think?"

"Is not a reason, is it?"

"No. But when Luciana was here she said almost the same thing. 'I want him so much I can hardly breathe.' The important question with my granddaughter is: Will she change her mind in a day, or a week? She is very young. Very impatient. Very impetuous. You need time to get to know each other. But if you two are alone without someone else present I know what will happen. And Cardullo would strangle you bare-handed if he found out you had touched his daughter."

Guido went back to his job. When he was working he was able to think calmly about plans for the future. He did not miss Italy as much as he had. English was becoming second nature to him. He could see himself staying on in America, settling here, pursuing his trade, perhaps even getting to be well-to-do. This was a place where anyone willing to work hard could succeed. Compared to Castiglion Fiorentino, Boston offered opportunities of every sort. One didn't even have to be skilled. There were jobs going begging everywhere, if you weren't too proud.

With marriage, another advantage emerged - there would be no difficulty about staying in America. Marriage to an American citizen would give him the option of remaining here indefinitely, if he wanted. He might even become a citizen himself. Would he want to? That was another kind of question. Do you renounce the land of your birth? It's not like putting off one coat to put on another. It's more a denial of loyalty to something that is yourself. A betrayal in a sense. But a few papers shuffled around and signed don't constitute betrayal. That was putting it too strongly. You did what was expeditious. If signing some papers got you something you wanted, what was changed? It didn't change you. You were still the same person. Or were you?

These thoughts troubled Guido. He could not escape a feeling that there was something inherently wrong, deceitful perhaps, in giving up a fundamental part of one's heritage. Well, it was not a step he need decide on at this time. Other things must come first.

He returned to the Cardullo's other evenings. Cardullo was a Red Sox fan. Guido quickly caught on to the way the game of baseball was played and found himself liking to listen to the radio.

The brother Paolino was rarely at home after supper and he never came in before Guido left. Marcello, a heavy, slow-moving, saturnine type, would go to his room after eating. He was studying accounting, they said. Guido could not say if he liked him or not. There was a quiet stubbornness about the man. Perhaps the father had pushed him too hard when a boy and he had retreated into silence and study, building a wall between himself and the blustering nearly illiterate father whom he had disappointed.

If a night game was being broadcast, Guido and Cardullo would listen while Luciana and her mother cleaned up the kitchen.

There was a thing about mothers and daughters that struck Guido. He remembered his own mother and Franca and how they would tidy up together and never stop chattering. They could talk without stopping when together, irritation turning to argument often enough, but another subject always crowding in to take over. Chit-chat, or gossip, or decisions about things needing to be done, they were never silent.

But Luciana liked baseball too, and often she would get just as excited as her father when the Red Sox would come from behind. She would join the two men in front of the radio and exhort the players with the same enthusiasm her father and Guido displayed.

One Sunday the three of them went to Fenway and saw the Sox beat the Yankees in a game that went into extra innings.

Guido was able to relax completely with Cardullo that day. Luciana sat between them and cheered or berated the players by turns. They ate popcorn and ice cream and drank Coca Cola and came back to the North End as tired as if they had played the entire game themselves.

To a limited degree Guido became a member of the family. Cardullo eyed him with supicion from time to time, but for the most part, accepted him. The two brothers at first cynically assumed they knew what Guido was after, but before long both came to regard him as someone who was not a threat to any of them. They saw the way their sister looked at Guido and were glad she was happy.

It was the mother who was slowest to show Guido any warmth. He was aware of her presence every time he came to the apartment the way you know that a house has a roof over it. If it were not there, it would not be a house. Yet you don't think about it. She was a force in the family. She was the mortar which held the structure together. Where the others might be morose or ebullient, bellicose or apathetic, she was a constant. Each depended upon her, always had. It was inconceivable that she had ever failed anyone in her family in time of need.

Where did her strength come from? If she needed help, if doubts assailed her, to whom did she turn? Guido did not know the answer. She did not ask for help from Don Tito, he was certain. Was her faith in God enough?

Cardullo and Paolino were both out, one evening. Marcello was closed in his room. A neighbor came upstairs and asked Luciana to watch her baby for half an hour while she went out for some medicine. Guido was left alone with Luciana's mother. They sat at the big oval table sipping *espresso*. The radio, for once, was turned off.

"Do you miss your family?" Luciana's mother asked.

"There are times when I miss them terribly."

For an awkward moment neither found anything else to say. Then Guido said: "You know, of course, that Luciana and I are thinking seriously about getting married."

"She has told me."

"You will say we are both very young, I suppose."

Guido hoped she would pick up on the phrase and tell him what her feelings were, but she sat silent, holding back. Maybe the departure of her daughter was a thing she feared. In that moment she would be left alone with her three men and no woman to talk to anymore. Then the boys would leave too, at least Paolino would. It would be a bad time for her. Did she hope it would never come?

"I was seventeen when I married," she said at last. "Luciana is a year older and knows far more about life than I did at that time. It is better for her to be married than to wait. I've seen the young men who have pursued her. They are not serious. What would become of her in a year or two more, if you and she do not marry, I don't wish to think. She loves you. This is not just the infatuation I have seen in her other times. She has grown up a great deal lately. Many things she does not tell me now. That hurts, but it is part of becoming herself.

"I want to tell you something, Guido Bussatti. I think marriage to you could be the best thing possible for Luciana. For you, though, I am not sure. I must be honest. You are young, as you have said. You are new to the way of life of America. You are new to being deeply in love. There is much growing up still ahead for you. Maybe Luciana has grown as much as she will."

He heard her but he did not believe her. He was sure that if he was going to go on discovering and learning, Luciana would do so too, along with him. Quickly he put aside the warning, but he responded to the frankness and the interest in him that Luciana's mother had shown. He began to see, not only the gentle strength in her, but also the great kindness and understanding. She was Don Tito's daughter after all. Wouldn't Luciana live under the same sign?

"Tell me about your mother," he asked.

She shook herself slightly, not having followed his train of thought.

"My mother? How to tell you about her? We were nine children. She had no time for anything but her family - her husband, Don Tito, and her children. She came from Cefalù, where my father found her. She grew up in seclusion. Her family had many possessions, many lands. Don Tito courted her because she was rich. Much later, he discovered what a prize she was, he says. She was only fifteen when she married. You see, 'young' can be very young.

"They came to the United States and eventually settled here in the North End where all of us children grew up. There were many hard years. My mother never rested. She just used herself up until there was nothing left and then she died. One day she was gone and I hadn't known her yet."

"You were thinking of this when you asked if I missed my family, weren't you?"

"I think of my mother often. Innocenza was her name. Such a name! Innocent she was when she married, brought up in a convent, protected and sheltered for fifteen years. And then? By the time she died was she innocent of any hardship, of any heartbreak, or any tragedy life can hold? She gave all of herself to all of us, but who remembers if she loved the fragrance of orange trees in blossom in the Sicily of her childhood or what she dreamed of when she was a young girl? Sometimes Don Tito talks of her. He's a good man, my father. As strong as my mother and clever too. But if I ask him how she did her hair when she was young, can he tell me?

"The Bible says: 'Honor thy mother and thy father.' More important would be to know and remember. We only learn that when it is too late."

Luciana came back into the apartment. "Whatsmatta?" she

asked, seeing them at the table, silent and unsmiling.

Guido looked up. "Your mother was telling me a little about <u>her</u> mother."

"I never knew my grandmother," Luciana said.

Her mother took a deep breath and sighed. "That's just what <u>I</u> was saying. I didn't know her either. Not enough. Nowhere near enough."

"Come on, Ma. That's not so. You were more than twenty, maybe twenty-five, before she died. Of course you knew her."

"I knew a woman who worked to feed us and to clothe us and to give us a clean place in which to live. I knew a woman who never lay down. The times we were alone together it was I who talked about me. Did I listen to what she may have told me? Did I ask her about herself? Did I ever hear the voice of the child she had once been and the dreams of that child? I don't think I took the trouble to ask. If I did, if I heard, I forgot."

She got up from the table. "I'll go to bed now. Come soon, Luciana. Don't let your father come home and find you two alone here."

She went down the hall. They heard her go into the bathroom and close the door.

Guido stood up and Luciana stepped inside his embrace. Alone with her, he forgot all else. His hands moved on her lithe back, descended to her waist and rose again along her sides so that the heel of each hand brushed her full breasts. She put her hands over his and pressed them to her.

"It's too much," he said. He drew away from her.

She stood in the center of the pink linoleum, her empty hands in the air still cupping the hands that had caressed her. "Oh Guido," she said. "How long must we wait?"

"I'll find a little apartment this week, Luciana. Then I'll ask your father if I may marry you."

They kept their voices low,

"I don't want to stay in Boston," she said.

"But my job is here."

"You can find work anywhere you go. I can work too. I want to get away from this place."

She said it with a vehemence that startled him. Before, he hadn't sensed her impatience with surroundings he had come to accept.

"Where would we go?" he asked.

"Anywhere," came the immediate reply. "I need to be free. I want us to start a new life on our own."

There was good sense in that. He could see that near her family she would be inhibited in many ways. So would he. But there was a cushion of security here too - friends, relatives, a known environment. As well as his job - something sure and adequate, at least for the moment.

"If we had our own place we'd be free, wouldn't we?"

"That wouldn't be enough. All this North End is a trap. Don't you see? Even the ones who get out - half go to East Boston, half to Revere. They take it with them. They don't ever escape."

Guido was puzzled. "Do you have such a need to escape?" There was something here he did not understand.

"I don't know," she said. "I know I want to get away. Far enough away not to get pulled back."

"Should I think of a place like New York?"

For a second she seemed to be trying to imagine that. Then she shook her head. "New York would be exciting, but it would be another city. I want to go where we can see the stars at night, where there will be trees and fields and flowers."

"Will there be work for me in such a place? I don't want to be just a farmer."

"You'll find work any place we go," she said again.

"If we are going away from Boston, I must know where before I speak to your father. This will mean a delay. And I have no idea where to begin to look. Have you any idea?"

She did. She stepped to him and took his hands in hers. "Several years ago, in the summer, I went for a week with an uncle and his family to a place on Cape Cod called Truro. You don't know how beautiful it was. We drove all over Cape Cod. There is everything there. We'll go there."

Had she been anyplace else? Did she know anything about conditions in this place she had seen as a tourist, a vacationer? Would it be expensive to live there? Was she right that he would find work?

He saw the chance to please her and all other considerations lost importance. "I'll go and look," he said.

Something hovered in the back of his mind. Then he remembered. The young man in the truck who had given him a ride. Where had he been headed? Wasn't it a place called Wellfleet on Cape Cod? And did he have any doubts about finding a niche there? None at all.

"I can go this week-end," Guido said. "I could leave Friday noon, if there's a bus, and come back for Monday noon. I'll catch up on work at night after I'm back. Could you get me some maps of Cape Cod tomorrow? And bus schedules to get there and back?"

He was almost laughing. "You are right, Luciana. We will do well to start someplace on our own. Just the two of us. So that everything will depend upon us, no one else."

The bus reached Hyannis a little after noon. Guido quickly found a place where he rented a bicycle. The deposit seemed pretty steep, but he'd get it back when he returned to the shop.

He hadn't ridden since leaving home. This bike was a better one than he'd had in Italy but it was different. He had to adjust the height of the seat before taking off, and then it took a while to get used to the different speeds. The old wreck he'd pedaled to Arezzo and back on so many times did not have any system for changing leverage as terrain changed.

He didn't spend much time in Hyannis. It was full of summer people. There were too many shops and too many cars - not at all the kind of place where he thought he would want to stay - so he took off down the road toward a town called Chatham.

To be rolling along again under his own power - a little effort, a lot of speed, the wind on his skin - what a pleasure. The bike had twin baskets over the rear wheel. His belongings were in them. His shirt too.

So this was the famous Cape Cod - an odd name that. He'd found out that the Cod was a codfish and a state symbol. He'd tried eating it one evening in Boston at a place on Washington Street. He thought it had about as much taste as a boiled roll of tissue paper, but perhaps he was unfair. A good cook would probably be able to give it some life.

There were no mountains on Cape Cod. In one pamphlet Luciana had given him, the author said the highest point on the Cape was only a little over two hundred feet above sea level.

Guido's home in Castiglion Fiorentino was higher than that above the main road. These were not even hills, just gentle rises with a long glide on the far side. In no time he reached Chatham.

Here was something he liked - salt water inlets and harbors poking sea-fingers inland, ponds and marshes everywhere. And he saw the houses he'd read about and for which the Cape was famous - old ones, eaves down to the level of the top of a man's head, big central brick chimneys, small windows with many lights, a similarity among them that you could easily identify, yet every one different.

Because the authentic old Capes, he had read, were hand-built, their timbers hand-hewn, additions and alterations made as needs changed and as materials became available. Fieldstone foundations followed the contours of the plot the houses grew on, and sloping shingled roofs, over the years, had dipped here and domed there as the buildings settled and old wood bent or stiffened with age.

Near a place where small boats were moored, he bought an order of fried clams and had a chocolate milk shake to go with them. - If I liked beer, he thought, I could pass for an American already. The clams had the taste of the sea in them.

There were still three hours of daylight. He looked at his map and decided to go on to Eastham. What was this 'ham' on the end of so many place names? Ham was pork, wasn't it? But it was also a part of the back of the leg. This English was terrible. Then he thought of the British use of the word 'hamlet.' Perhaps that explained it...things that go through your head when you're riding a bicycle, the road trailing away behind you and anything, everything still waiting ahead.

He wasn't tired yet. He might even make it to Wellfleet, where that other young man was headed months ago. But Guido knew he'd be stiff the next day. Better not keep going too long.

When the sun went down he was just passing Lieutenant Island

Road. Pitch pine and scrub oak lined the roadside. Traffic had thinned out. There were no reflectors on the bike and there was no light. Guido passed a place that had cabins for rent but a No Vacancy sign hung at the entrance to the drive. Another half hour passed before he found a place to spend the night. It was expensive, but it was quiet. A hot shower relaxed his tightening muscles. He ate bread and cheese he had brought with him, had an orange for dessert and fell asleep the moment he stretched out on the bed.

Something woke him. For a moment he was confused. Then he remembered where he was and saw by his watch that it was almost four in the morning. A sound reached him, a wavering descending note, not a whistle, but almost.

Only the faintest pale light of dawn filtered through the pines beyond the window. The quavering gentle note came again. Was it a bird? An owl? In the country, at home, at dusk and often near dawn, an owl called, a little fellow, seldom seen. They called him the *chiu*, like the letter 'Q.' He had only the one note, not the tremolo this bird was sounding. Were the two related?

Guido pulled on his clothes and stepped outside. The bird was gone, at least it didn't call again. In the early stillness there was the distant shush of small waves breaking on a beach. The air was cool and sweet, pine-scented and clean.

He went back inside and put his things together. He'd already paid. Ten minutes later he was pedaling north again, no cars on the road, morning light increasing quickly, bringing every tree into sharp outline, colors beginning to show where there had been only shadows minutes before, the world awakening.

Close to the road in a marshy inlet, he came on a doe. She had been feeding there, lifted her head to study this figure on two wheels spinning toward her, froze for an instant, then went bounding away, long glorious arcs air-borne and effortless. Had she marveled, too, for that split second before going, at the swift easy silent way Guido was moving?

He came to the turn off for Wellfleet as the sun was rising and decided to explore the center of town, followed his nose and came out by the docks and the harbor, boats tied up there, all kinds of boats, small ones and larger ones. He had no names for them. It didn't matter.

A man with a long rake and a wire basket was seated on a piling by the water. The tide had been out and was coming back in. The man was opening some kind of shell with a stubby knife. When the upper half was free, he dropped it into the water and then seemed to inhale the raw mollusk and the juices on the other half. A look of pure happiness overspread his face as he masticated slowly and then swallowed.

"You ever eat a raw oyster, Son?" the man asked Guido, when he saw him watching.

"I never have," Guido answered.

"Like ta try?"

"What is it like?"

"Never met anyone yet could tell me that. Y'aren't squeamish are ya?"

"Squeamish? I don't know. I've heard that these 'oysters' are a delicacy."

The man opened another and offered it to Guido. Guido propped his bicycle against the nearest piling. He accepted the gift with some misgivings. The gray body of the oyster quivered on the shell in his hand. He raised it to his lips and sucked the slippery amorphous glob into his mouth. Its consistency almost made him change his mind. Then he began to chew and the mingling of soft meat and marine juices was like nothing he had ever had before. He swallowed. This was a bit of Nature's bounty he would never forget.

"Like it?" the man asked.

"Exquisite," Guido said. "Do you...collect these somewhere

here?"

"Dig 'em, Son. Gotta know where. An' when. Want another?"

"I would. But what could I give you in return?"

"Little wine'd go good with these. Just jokin.'"

"Quite by chance," Guido said, "I have a bottle of wine with me." He rummaged in his baskets and brought out a bottle of Chianti. "This looks like a perfect time to see if this is still good."

The man was eyeing Guido with respect, perhaps even with affection.

They sat side by side on the ramp, perched like gaunt gulls on old pilings. An oyster. A jolt of red. The jug went back and forth.

A fisherman came along the wharf. "Kinda early, ain't it, Charlie?" he said.

"Satidy, ain't it," Charlie answered.

Guido had some Italian bread with him. They shared that too. When the wine was gone there were still a lot of oysters left. Guido could not remember a more substantial or satisfying breakfast.

"You had enough?" Charlie asked him.

"You have given me a new experience, Mr. Charlie."

"Glad you come along, Son."

They got to their feet. With a certain amount of formality they shook hands and parted. Guido glided out of town filled with contentment, the bike rolling effortlessly, sunlight inside and out.

For an hour, in Truro, he followed side roads, then came to a spot where the Atlantic lay at the base of an escarpment more than fifty feet high, long combers rolling toward him, curling and cresting, then thudding onto the sand. It could have been this place that Luciana remembered. He understood how it must have delighted her. This was the other end of the world from the crowded North End of Boston. But could he make a living here?

He kept going and by midday was approaching Provincetown. The stiffness he'd felt earlier was gone - no doubt the wine had helped - and he felt he could ride on until nightfall.

Dunes were drifting over the road at one point, then a lake appeared on his right, cabins on the Bay side. Up ahead he could see a kind of tower, a 'monument' someone had told him, a bad imitation of an Italian structure, a sort of Palazzo Vecchio without being old, or a palace.

Then he was walking the bike down a street crowded with tourists and artist types. The scene was familiar somehow. Somewhere in Italy he'd been in a crowd like this one once before. Where was it? In Florence? But here the odd ones seemed to have made a special effort to look as outrageous as possible. It was scarcely more than noon but a woman was coming toward him wearing a formal gown, turquoise and rust. Black gloves came to her elbows. Blue eye-shadow and pancake make-up made a mask of her face. A wig and a floppy-brimmed hat seemed part of a costume. Was she a walking advertisement for a show? Was she...? Under the make-up he made out the shadow of a beard. *Che roba ragazzi!*

The shops were intriguing. They were all sorts, most with specialties. Like the residents, each tried to be different. New products in ramshackle buildings, modern art and pepperoni pizza, book stores and fishing tackle, haberdasheries and health food - a shacky-tacky studied decadence along with a long-standing proud tolerance of diversity.

He liked it. He liked the special cachet of the seaside resort, the small port, a place where there were boats and a wharf and a tide always coming or going, filling the air with sea smells - mud flats and fish odors.

But he couldn't see himself making a living in Provincetown. What happened in the wintertime in this place? What was its population when all the gawpers were gone? For that matter, what did the tourists want that he could provide even when they abounded?

He had chowder in a sort of bar and then headed out of town, back some of the way he had come.

All day he rode at a steady pace, more than anything delighting in the pure physical joy of using his body. The air was clean on the Cape. The sun on his bare back and shoulders burned a little and felt good.

Instead of returning to Chatham, he took the road into Brewster and followed 6A along the Bay so that by late afternoon he reached Barnstable Village. A sign in front of a three-story building said Guests. He took a room for the night. His bike was safe in a barn at the rear of the house. He cleaned up and went walking.

Main Street, the part where the shops were, was not much longer than the distance you could kick a soccer ball. The old Barnstable County Courthouse dominated one end. It was an imposing stone building, granite, it seemed, but the four massive columns of the portico could not have been granite. They were all of a piece. Guido approached and tapped them and found out they were wood, cleverly disguised as gray stone.

Two iron cannons flanked the walk up to the entrance. They were mounted in stone. No one was going to walk off with them.

Some stores, a restaurant, a Post Office, the Courthouse - that was the Village. A white church spire was visible beyond a four corners. The road at that crossing led down to a small marina. Guido walked there, past a burial ground and a house that was as long as a tunnel.

Small power boats were moored in the marina, some, larger, for charter. Gulls turned over the spillway into the marsh at his right. Small fish were breaking there. The gulls were dropping on them, screaming, their hollow cries filling the evening air with the sound of voracious feeding and squabbling.

Farther on, was a small beach overlooking the harbor, and across the harbor Guido saw a long point of land with the base of a lighthouse standing near its tip.

The sun was going down. He walked back to the Village, bought things to eat at the general store and went to his room for supper. When he finished, he went out again and found a pay phone.

He didn't like to use the phone. Somehow, the hardest thing of all, in this second language, was to speak into a mouthpiece and understand what was said through a part next to your ear. Luckily it was Luciana who answered.

"I've been waiting and waiting for you to call," she said.

"I'm sorry. I've been riding a bicycle for two days. I think I've covered about two hundred kilometers."

"Did you see Truro?"

"I stood on a high dune, I think it is called that, and underneath me the open ocean came seething up the beach. There were huge waves. It was beautiful."

"Will we live there, do you think?"

"I don't know, Luciana. It might be difficult to earn any money there."

"What else have you seen?"

"I've been in Hyannis, where the bus went, and Chatham and Orleans and Wellfleet and Truro and Provincetown. Guess what. They call Provincetown Peetown! And I went through Brewster and Yarmouth. Tonight I'm in Barnstable Village."

"Do you miss me?"

"I would ride all the way back to Boston tonight, just to be with you for an hour."

"First decide where we are going to live."

"The voice of reason. Are you alone?"

"Pop went to bed early, if that's what you mean."

"*Ti amo, Luciana*...I love you."

"That sounds pretty in both languages. I love you too."

"Tomorrow I'll try to find out what work there is here. I'll talk to people."

"Don't talk to any other girls."

"Hey. I'll tell you about a girl I saw in Peetown."

"You better not."

"No. Listen. She was wearing an evening gown, in the middle of the day. She had make-up all over her face, and big eyelashes. And she was a man."

"I hate to think what Pop would do if he met someone like that. We better not live in that place."

"I'll find us something. Trust me. I'll be back Monday noon. Come to the shop at lunch hour. Okay?"

"I'll be there. Be careful."

"You too. *Buona notte, Luciana.*"

"Goodnight, Guido."

He replaced the phone. Her husky voice still whispered in his ear. He would have given a year off his life just to hold her in that moment.

The lady who ran the guest house was up before Guido the next morning. She served him corn muffins and coffee and orange juice when he came down the stairs.

"Will you be staying another night?" she asked.

"I'm not sure," Guido answered. He told her why he had come to the Cape and what work he did.

"You could do worse than settle here," she said. "I've enough things need doing in this house and the barn to keep you busy a long time. Do you do carpentry too?"

"I don't know much about construction work, but I can do almost anything else that has to do with working with wood."

She had something in mind and Guido thought she'd put it into words if he gave her enough time.

"You're a foreigner, aren't you," she said.

"I am Italian, yes. But I will be getting married soon. To an American."

"And it's you and your future wife will need a place to live?"

"Just as soon as I can find something."

"Not in a family way, is she?"

The question took Guido by surprise. He was not used to such outspoken ways. Should he be offended? "We are not yet married," he replied, a bit coolly.

The lady hesitated. "If I spoke out of turn," she said, "please forgive me." She paused.

"I've been thinking for some time that if I fixed an apartment in the barn I could rent it and get my money back in only a couple of years. There's plumbing out there already. It's primitive as it stands now, but if you and your wife, when you are married, were to take it and fix it up the way it ought to be, you could have a place to live until next summer. I'd want it ready to rent and vacant by next June first, but until then it could be yours."

"Is that the barn where I put my bicycle last night?"

"Yes."

"And the upper part..."

"The loft."

"The loft is a sort of apartment already?"

"Let me show it to you."

They went through the kitchen and out the back door. The bicycle was in the lower part of the barn where Guido had seen furniture and garden equipment and an old truck and cases containing no-telling-what. There was a sturdy outside stairway to the loft. They climbed it. A new roof had been put on the barn only a few years before. The lady opened a wide door with a key and they stepped into what had once been a place for storing hay. There was even a faint lingering fragrance, salty somehow. Had it been marsh hay, bales of it, stacked here for decades and decades?

"There are mice here now," the lady said. "Your wife may not like that. Maybe if you had a cat you could control them.

"As you can see, there's a toilet and a sink, for washing. I rented to some very bohemian types once. They loved it, but they didn't do me any good. I thought if we put in a proper bathroom with a toilet, a shower stall and a washbowl, and if we had a proper kitchen next to the bath, then the rest would not be very hard to arrange."

The space was considerable, about ten by fifteen meters, Guido estimated. The floor, at the two sides, was barely four feet lower than the eaves so that the windows there went from baseboard level to the place where the roof and the wall met. There would be no easy way to change that.

"My idea was to partition this to create two bedrooms." The lady indicated where they should be. "With the bath and a big walk-in closet here, that would leave all the rest of the area for an open living room-diningroom-kitchen. What do you think?"

Guido didn't dare to believe this was happening. "I think it could be wonderful," he said. "But you would need a *trombaio*. How do you say that? To make the tubing?"

"A plumber. Yes. I have someone to do that."

"And an electrician. Maybe he could do electric heat. I've heard that is easy to install."

"I have an electrician who has worked for me."

"And would you pay for all the materials?"

"I would. I'd need to be sure, though, that you could do all the other work and do it well."

Guido could see it already. "This is a special kind of work," he said, "very well suited to me. You see, nothing here is at right angles. Nothing is level. This barn is a beauty and sound, but he has leaned a little. I will have to make many extra cuts to fit floors and rafters and partitions in place.

"I could make drawings, today, if you have a tape measure, and estimate some of the material - quantity that is, not price, because I have little knowledge so far of costs here."

He was trying to think ahead. This looked like a rare opportunity.

"I must return to Boston before Monday noon. I could phone you, after you think it over, after you speak with your plumber and electrician, and you could say then if you want to proceed."

"We should write out an agreement, if we go ahead."

"I would like that."

The lady was studying him. What was she thinking? She must have been on her own for a long time. She was accustomed to making decisions, that seemed clear.

"I'll go get you a tape," she said, "and paper and pencil to make drawings. I'll be back in a minute."

She left. When she returned, she had a clipboard with her as well as the other items. "While you're working here," she said, "I'll try to write out an agreement. At noon you'll have lunch with me and we'll go over it."

He was alone again. He spread his arms and took a deep breath. This big barn was going to be the first home he would give to Luciana and he would have a major part in shaping it. It would be special in many ways. She would see what he was capable of doing.

But first he had to deal with working in feet and inches. What a clumsy foolish way to measure things. The tape, though, gave him no choice.

He set about the task of drawing a floor plan. It turned out to be more complicated than he'd thought. The west wall was nine inches longer than the east wall. The north and south walls were not parallel. Whoever had built the barn, apparently, had simply set stones on four corners, squinted, judged it good enough, and started building.

Materials were another difficult matter. Guido was unsure what many things were called. He didn't know what was available either. Insulation, wallboard, nail sizes and types - he needed to spend a day in a lumberyard to learn nomenclature and quality. Well, that would come soon enough. At Panaschi's he had become familiar with a fair share of what he'd need. He wrote descriptions of what he thought he'd require. A supplier would understand - and probably would come up with what Guido wanted.

The agreement the lady prepared was straightforward. Guido and Luciana, once lawfully married, would have a place to live, rent free, until the first day of the following June. They would pay their own electric bills. The new electric service would be in place within one month. Guido was expected to do all the work of converting the loft into a desirable apartment. Appliances would be paid for by the owner. All plumber's and electrician's fees were hers too.

"You know," the lady said, "legally this document doesn't have much value. I've found that even contracts drawn up by expensive lawyers are worth little more than the paper they're written on. The only really important thing, the only binding ingredient, is the good will of the parties. I will do everything I reasonably can to make this a profitable and favorable venture for you. I trust you will take the same attitude in my regard."

Guido was moved by her words. It was good to have something in writing, a statement of general intent, but he realized, even before he saw what she had written, that there would be no way to foresee all possible contingencies in an agreement of this sort. He did not doubt for a moment that he could count on her good will. "I will do everything I can," he told her, "to make certain that you are not disappointed."

"*Carissimi, sono tornato per l'ultima volta nella mia stanzina di Beacon Hill*...Dearest ones, I have returned for the last time to my tiny room on Beacon Hill. Tomorrow I will be married. This comes for you, I know, as a shock. I have not written you before of the young woman I am about to marry. This is not because I have not wanted to. It is because my words can only convey a meager part of the emotion, the love, I feel for Luciana. To attempt to describe her to you would be futile. I can only say - she is beautiful. I will send you a photograph as soon as I can.

"My job in the North End, finished today. I have saved a little money, enough to carry us, Luciana and me, for a couple of months at least. We will be going to live in the top of a big barn in a town called Barnstable on Cape Cod. That is about one hundred and twenty kilometers south of Boston.

"For a month, week-ends, I have worked on the barn to convert it to an apartment for us. The lady who owns it will let us live there until next June, rent free, in return for the work I have done and have still to do. This is very favorable since rents are unbelievably high here. Luckily, wages are just as high. Everything is in proportion.

"I expect to be able to earn a living in Barnstable. There are many who do carpentry here, and construction. And they are very good. Very efficient. But fine work - cabinet making, inlay - these crafts are at a premium. Who knows? Perhaps I will become rich and famous. Then I can send you tickets to come to visit me in a luxurious mansion! Just dreaming.

"The important thing is that tomorrow Luciana and I begin a life together. To tell the truth, I am as nervous as a chickadee.

"The family of my bride is like an army and some of them regard me with suspicion. I don't know what many of them do for a living. America has ways I have not understood as yet. Luciana's grandfather, Don Tito di Montefalcone, comes from Sicily. He is a stern wise man and has been my friend. Luciana's mother is strong like a mountain. Her husband, Francesco Cardullo, is strong like a bull.

"Luciana is the one who has said we should get away from her family and begin a life of our own. I think she is right. That is why I went to Cape Cod to find a place where we will not be under the influence of her family. You can see, she is an independent person. Even though this is the case with her family, I would not have wanted to separate myself from the three of you if you had been here. And yet...it is probably a good thing for a new couple to make their own beginnings.

"Well, tomorrow is the fateful day. My life will not be the same again. Send us your love and your blessing. Nothing else.

"I send you all my love and hope that we can all five be together someday before too long. *Un abbraccione. Buona notte. Guido.*"

The church was packed. Probably everyone present would become a relative by marriage. It was a frightening thought. Guido had been introduced to aunts and uncles and nephews and nieces until his head was spinning. He gave up any effort to remember who was who. The brothers and sisters of Luciana's mother, and the spouses and children and parents of spouses, counted over three score. Then there were all the members of the Cardullo family. There were even a few ex-wives and stepchildren - church or no church. A veritable battalion. Small wonder Luciana wanted to flee. On the other hand, with the closeness that they showed each other, what would anyone have to fear from the outside world? The National Guard could not have turned out in any more impressive array.

Luciana, dressed all in white, in a gown altered only slightly that her grandmother, Don Tito's wife, had worn for her marriage, was so lovely that many of those swarthy southern Italian faces turned to look at Guido with envy, even resentment.

The rental suit he was wearing made him uncomfortable. The tight bow tie, the black shoes that pinched his feet, the narrow-waisted pants - all chafed and tormented him. He liked loose-fitting clothes. But he knew he was much admired. If dark looks reached him, looks of longing did too. There were some sultry beauties among his relatives-to-be.

The priest was a rotund burly jovial type who enjoyed the marriage ceremony but didn't linger over it. He knew, from past experience, that a bounteous reception would follow. Perhaps that's where his mind was.

He pronounced the couple man and wife. Guido turned to face Luciana. He kissed her lightly, self-conscious before so many strangers and his lowering father-in-law. Everyone was watching. Luciana handed her corsage to her father, then put both arms around Guido's neck. A cheer went up. It sounded like the crowd at a prize fight in the Arena when a good blow is landed. - Well, Guido thought, why not, the knockout punch has been thrown now. Smiling, laughing, relaxing, he let the moment lift him and carry him. She was his now. They would be happy.

The reception was in a rented hall. The quantity of food and wine, pastries and special dishes and hard liquor was staggering. The cost must have been in the thousands of dollars.

Children were everywhere. A band played "O Sole Mio" and "Come Back to Sorrento" and many old Sicilian songs. A man who must have thought of himself as a tenor grabbed the microphone and tried to sing, but he kept forgetting the words. The band did its best to drown him out.

At a table with four other old men, sat Don Tito. He signaled Guido to come to him. Guido pushed through the crowd. He was stopped again and again. His hand was shaken, he was clapped on the back, he was poked in the ribs.

"Guido Bussatti," Don Tito said, "I wish you good fortune. This is a day of great joy for you. I hope your joy may be carried forward far into the future. But if you encounter difficulties I will be honored to have you remember me and bring your troubles to me while I am still here."

He handed Guido an envelope. "Put this in a safe place," he said. "Now go back to your bride. And be good to her."

Someone else had taken over the microphone. It was one of the uncles. Onofrio was his name. He was making a speech, but not many were listening.

Surrounding Luciana was a circle of grim-faced older women.

They retreated as Guido approached.

"None too soon," Luciana said. "A little longer and they would have had me asking for an annulment."

"I'll get a razor and cut off their tongues."

"I think they would like to cut off something else."

He touched her cheek gently. "You're not afraid, are you?"

"Of course not," she said. "You better be afraid of me."

"Should I really?"

"You have married a woman who will never leave you alone."

"That's what I wanted."

"Maybe you'll change your mind."

"Nothing can make me change my mind about you."

Luciana's mother appeared beside them. "I've packed a basket of things for you to eat," she said.

"How soon can we slip away?" Luciana asked.

"Anytime now. Some of those Taglis have had too much to drink already. I hope they don't make trouble. Maybe they'll go home after you leave."

Bruno Tagli had married one of Cardullo's sisters. He worked for the DPW and would have lost his job a dozen times, but he had connections that made him immune from removal. Until he killed someone, or until someone killed him, he was untouchable.

"If I don't get a chance to tell you before you go..." She was weeping. Luciana kissed her mother. Guido touched his lips to her wide smooth forehead. "May God be with you," she said, and turned away.

They made for a side door and were able to get out without being noticed. Paolino was waiting for them in a Chevvy coupe. He drove them to the apartment where they changed and collected their belongings. Then he brought them back to the hall.

Out front was parked the near-new Ford pick-up truck that Cardullo had given them as a wedding present. It was loaded with gifts as well as many of the things they would need.

Guido had only acquired a license the week before, but driving was second nature to him. After Italy's cities, even Boston's insane traffic held no terrors for him.

The whole crowd came out to see them off. Cardullo shoved his way through to them. He kissed Luciana. Then he looked at Guido. There were tears on his face. He gave Guido a punch on the upper arm hard enough to hurt and then enclosed him in a bear hug and let him go. "Take care of my little girl," he said.

The truck backfired twice when it started. Everyone yelled. A hail of rice and confetti struck their chariot and they were off. They were on the road. They were on their own.

It was a two hour trip to the Cape and just getting out of Boston from the North End took some special maneuvering. Guido concentrated on the driving and Luciana, close against him, was unusually quiet. But when they crossed the bridge onto Cape Cod she seemed to wake up.

"Aren't you hungry?" she asked.

He hadn't thought about food. The basket of things to eat was on the seat beside Luciana. "I'm hungry," he said, "but let's wait until we get to our new home. It's only a little way now."

"Is there a door to the bathroom yet?"

"That was one of the last things I did. Let's just hope the electrician got the hot water heater connected."

"How about plates, and silverware? I never thought..."

"Your mother was going to give us those. Maybe they are packed in the back."

"If not, we'll eat with our fingers."

"I can stand that."

Luciana was quiet again for a spell, then she said: "It's a little bit scary, isn't it? It's just the two of us now."

"That's what you wanted, I think."

"Yes. I'm glad about that. But you saw. Pop was crying. I never saw him cry before in all my life. That big tough old father of mine was crying to see us go away. Ma too. But I knew she'd cry. Not Pop."

"He was remembering, maybe," Guido said.

"Remembering what?"

"Remembering the day he and your mother started out."

Luciana didn't answer.

They drove through Sandwich and past the road to Sandy Neck. There were marshes to their left. The July afternoon was heavy with sea air and the fragrance of things flowering. Cattails by the roadside, like a forest of exclamation points, accentuated the level serenity of the marsh.

They came into Barnstable Village, past the County Courthouse, and then turned into the drive to the place where they would live.

"This is it," Guido said. He got out of the truck and so did Luciana. She looked at the place to which her husband had brought her. It was not what she had expected. No one she knew had ever lived in a place like this.

"Come," Guido said. "Let me show you the apartment. You could smile, you know."

"It's a barn," she said.

"Yes," he said. "It is. I told you it was. And it's very special. Come see." He grabbed two of the suitcases and led the way up the outside staircase. He got out his key and opened the door. They went inside.

The floors were unfinished. A pile of shavings remained where he had swept them into a corner. There were no cabinets yet in the kitchen. He had visualized it as it would be when finished - now he saw it as Luciana did.

He set down the suitcases. "You will see, Luciana. In no time, here, I will build cabinets that no one else has anywhere. These floors, these gorgeous wide boards, will be sanded and then coated with a new sort of varnish used on ships so that the warm ruddy-orange colors and textures of the old wood will come forth. We will paint the trim around the windows and doors. You will find materials for curtains. In a couple of weeks we will have a place you could write about and put in a magazine."

He held her in his arms. She softened. She caught some of his enthusiasm.

"Look around," he said. "I'll bring the rest of our things upstairs."

She checked the large new refrigerator. It was connected and working. The double sink with swing faucet had both hot and cold water. An electric stove was going to take some getting used to. They had gas in the North End. The bath was complete except for the floor, and doors for the cabinets. What was to be their bedroom had a double bed in it and a bureau. The closet lacked a door. No drapes covered the windows.

Guido came in with the last of their packages.

"We need tables and chairs and lamps - many things," Luciana said.

"Don't worry," Guido said. "Downstairs there are so many pieces of furniture to choose from you will never get through. The landlady has been stacking old stuff and broken things down there for years. She says we can use anything we want as long as I repair it. We'll go through it tomorrow and you can pick out what you want. I didn't want to get too much furniture up here before I do the floors because it would be in the way."

They were alone together at last. They were in their own quarters behind a door they could lock. Both were thinking of the night that lay ahead, that could even start now, in the afternoon.

"We should eat some of the good things Ma fixed for us," Luciana said, "and store the rest of it in the refrigerator."

A shyness had come over each of them. They avoided touching as they unpacked the picnic basket. They found sandwiches and fried chicken, a thermos of cold milk, a pecan pie and a chocolate cake, apples and oranges and grapes, a pound of butter, flour and sugar and salt and other seasonings, a dozen eggs. The perishables had been wrapped in waxed paper and then in newspapers, with ice cubes in plastic bags to keep everything cool.

In a carton they found a complete service of plates and saucers and soup bowls for six. Pots and pans were in another carton along with silverware.

"Your mother thought of everything," Guido said.

Luciana was shaking her head. "I had no idea she was doing all this. We'd be out looking for a hamburger stand if she hadn't."

They ate and then began putting some things away. Much would have to stay in cartons until shelves and closets were finished.

"It's early," Guido said. "Let's go for a walk. I'll show you the harbor and the Village. Then we can come back here."

They went out. They met the landlady who smiled on them and said if they needed anything at all to ask for it.

At the marina they watched a man in a blue cap with a visor crank his boat onto a trailer at the base of the ramp. Before he got in his truck to go he lifted the lid on the fish box in the open boat. They were watching from above and saw it was filled to the top with big fish, stripers, they learned later. The man said nothing, but they could see he was pleased with himself. He drove away, water draining from the scuppers, leaving a dark wet line on the roadway.

It was dusk when they returned to their apartment. Guido shut the door behind them and locked it. They stood against each other in the darkness, each holding the other, hands moving.

"You will be gentle with me?" Luciana asked.

"I will."

She drew away from him and went into the bathroom. He heard the shower running. When she came out he went in and showered in his turn.

In the bedroom she made up the bed with fresh sheets. There was no lamp there, but through the uncurtained window came enough light to see by.

He found her brushing her hair by the bureau. In the half light he could see she was wearing something filmy and transparent that only fell to the tops of her thighs. He was sure that her mother had not picked that out, had probably never seen it.

A towel was about his waist. It didn't conceal his excitement. He put his hands on her warm shoulders and she pressed her palms against his chest so that their bodies still didn't touch. Her fingers slipped lightly over his torso. Where she touched him his skin remained sensitized as if the air there were set whirling, miniature dust devils all over his body. She put a finger inside the towel and pulled and it dropped to the floor so that he was naked and she could see him.

He lifted the flimsy nightgown over her shoulders and placed it on the bureau, then let his eyes travel over her body. Breasts that full he had not dared imagine before. Her waist was small, her navel deep. Her dense pubic bush was an area of darkness and her long straight legs pale columns. He took her hand and they stepped to the bed and lay down side by side, still not touching - except for his hands that then moved on her lightly, learning the shapes of her.

She closed her eyes and let him look at her. When he filled his hands with her breasts she felt the nipples stiffen, caught her breath when his mouth took the place of his rough palm.

Down her sides and all over her body a prickling rising anticipation of yet more pleasure joined anxiety. With her eyes closed, she could not forget the size and the length of the erect organ she had stared at when the towel fell to the floor. Would there be pain with the pleasure?

He drew her against him so that they lay on their sides, the length of their bodies pressed together, her breasts against his chest, his member hard against the yielding mound of her belly, their legs enlaced. He ran his right hand down her back and over her full rounded hip.

They kissed. Their mouths were well known each to the other. While they were kissing he entered her.

She caught her breath. For a long moment she stopped breathing. She could tell some of the shape of that part of him by the way he filled her, could feel his hardness, clasp his warmth.

He, too, stopped breathing. They held each other and didn't move. He had feared some obstruction. There was none. Did that mean anything? Did it matter?

Slowly they began moving together. The faint light from the window revealed her face to him, eyes still closed but mouth partly open, lips shaped to kiss. Her black hair on the pillow shimmered and glistened.

She sensed a surface within her lifting like a wave coming ashore, far out but coming closer, taking form, another wave behind it.

He was over her and his lean frame moved on her, pressed on her lightly, most of his weight on forearms and knees. How could she have thought this would hurt her?

She seemed to be falling, falling backwards, falling into something softer than air but warm as a summer wind, the waves coming closer, beginning to crest, then leaning and breaking and breaking and breaking.

He saw the change in her expression, heard the gasp and the cry. He closed his eyes then and was aware of every place every part of him touched her, inside and out. He had held back. Now he held back no more. He felt the world folding in on itself, gathering for an explosion. There were flashes of light inside his head and a rushing sound like wind-blown sand on the side of a cabin. For a moment he was suspended in space, bodiless. Then he was earth-bound again, coming, bursting, splitting apart, shuddering to an emptiness, completed and spent.

That was one of the things about it that Guido couldn't get over. Why did the act of love leave you, at least momentarily, feeling annihilated - as if sex were the obliteration of being, not a creative act? As if it were the be-all and end-all of existence, at one and the same time. He didn't understand. Perhaps all that mattered in this life was to assure the continuation of the species. Was that it?

After he and Luciana had made love he could sink into a sleep so deep nothing could wake him. It was as close to a death as he wanted to come. It was peace, complete and total peace - for a while.

But as time went by they didn't make love as often as during that first year when they found release almost every night. In the daytime too. In the shower. Underwater, once when they borrowed a canoe and paddled up into the marsh where the water was warm and no one could see them.

Luna di miele it was called in Italian, same as in English. Honeymoon, moon of honey. Why?

That first year had been all honeymoon. Almost. As sweet as honey. All loving and love making.

He'd worked too. Every waking hour, practically. He'd finished their apartment before the end of August. It was a showplace, a labor of love. The landlady rented it now for more money than he made. Well, it had been a good deal for them too. Almost a year that they paid no rent. It had given Guido time to find the building on Main Street, just down from the Courthouse, to put it in shape and acquire the tools that he needed.

For a while they lived on the second floor and the shop was downstairs. Their first lease was for two years. Guido began making signs, hand-carved, and there seemed to be steady money there. The future looked calm and settled and predictable.

But in the months after Pierino was born, their life changed. Of course, having a child had to make a difference. You don't sleep through the night if there is a baby to be fed. If you haven't made love you sleep lightly. All routines are turned topsy-turvy.

Guido had expected that Luciana would nurse the baby herself. Breasts like hers surely should have served that purpose. But someone had told her they would sag and lose their shape if she breast-fed her child, so she put him on formula and as often as not it was Guido who had to get up in the night and change his son and feed him.

He didn't mind it, really. He loved the closeness it created between him and Pierino, those hours in the silence of the night when only the two of them were together, when he could hold his infant son and their eyes would lock. "Windows of the soul," was that it? He didn't know. He only knew that wordless and mysterious, there was communication between them in those moments. Broken sleep, though, left Guido tired in the daytime.

And Luciana complained, too, that their second home was not as nice as their first. Even of the first, she spoke with a trace of disdain. "The hay barn," she called it, as if it were a joke. But the joke didn't hide the fact that she had been a little ashamed of living in something that was not a bone fide house.

"When will we live in a proper home, like other people?" she asked.

"As soon as we get a little ahead I'll buy us a piece of land," Guido said.

"And how long will that take?"

"I don't know. We'll have to wait and see."

"Why don't we borrow the money?"

He wanted to please her. He knew of an acre of land off Bragg's Lane that was for sale. The next week he got a commitment from a bank and arranged the purchase. The bank lawyer found a flaw in the title. There had been a right of way across a corner of the property eighty years earlier. As a practical matter, Guido saw no way that anyone could exercise that right after so many years. The lawyer said that the bank would not give him the loan if there remained any cloud on the title. By the time this was taken care of, the lawyer's fees nearly equaled the price of the land.

Guido met a builder who hired him for Sundays and evenings. It was a way to learn rough framing, easy enough, and to earn some more money. Later, too, he did a lot of finish work for the builder. But it meant he was putting in as much as seventy hours a week between his own shop and the outside work. He paid off the bank, though. And the bank's slimy lawyer.

He went to a different bank and asked for a construction loan. He got it. But it required another title search by another lawyer and that charge would be added to the mortgage when he moved into the house later that year.

The interest rate seemed high. Guido asked if it might be adjusted downward.

"This is a 'spec' house," the banker told him.

"What does that mean?" Guido asked.

"You built it for speculation. You're going to sell it as soon as you get it done."

"That is not so," Guido said. "This will be my home. For me and my family. And it is finished now except for some small details."

"What about the place where you live now? That's not a home?"

The banker was about fifty. Overweight. He looked incapable

of smiling. And he didn't like foreigners.

- So if this is a 'spec' house, Guido thought, maybe I should sell it and let that banker be right.

Others were doing this sort of thing. Maybe he could clear five thousand dollars on a quick sale and have a stake for starting another home. He asked Luciana what she thought.

"Never," she said. "Now that we're ready to get out of these crummy three rooms you are not going to sell that house."

Was he wrong not to insist? It might have been a turning point. But he understood how much she wanted to have a real home of her own, how much she wanted to tell her family that at last she lived in a real house.

There was going to be a separate room for Pierino and a utility room with washer and dryer, a guest bedroom, a big living room, a complete kitchen, a bath upstairs and down - she was going to have what she had wanted for too long already. He gave in.

But the week they moved into the new house, she ordered a living room and bedroom set from Sears Roebuck without telling him. Guido came back to the house late, after a long day, and saw what she had chosen and couldn't believe it.

"What is this?" he demanded, when he walked in.

"Isn't it beautiful?" she asked.

"Where did it come from?"

"They delivered it today. From Sears."

"You bought this stuff?"

"It was a big sale. Forty per cent off."

"You used your charge?"

"Of course. What else? What are you acting this way about? I thought I would make you happy."

"Luciana, this is the kind of rubbish we spent all our time repairing at Panaschi's."

"Rubbish! How can you say that? Some of the best people in

Hyannis furnish their homes with this...this..."

"*Robaccia*."

"It is not *robaccia*. And stop always telling me things in Italian."

"We'll phone them to come and take it back."

"We will not. Do you want to make a fool of me?"

"I suppose I better ask you how much all this cost."

"It was a saving of eight hundred dollars."

"How much did it cost is what I want to know."

"There is even a free crib for Pierino."

"So we can throw away the one I built for him. Right? How much, Luciana? How much did you spend?"

"It was twelve hundred dollars. You haven't even seen the bedroom set."

"Twelve hundred dollars! *Dio benedetto*! And how will we ever pay that?"

"We have ninety days before the first payment is due."

"*Fantastico*! A supended sentence. Ninety days. With the mortgage on this house and the rent on the shop and maybe we might want to eat once a week? That's just wonderful."

It was their first real fight. Guido was too angry to think clearly. The antiques he would have brought to their home one at a time, the pieces he would have created, the unusual items he could have found and refurbished and made integral to their life, would not find a place here after all. It was as if she didn't know what he did for a living, put no value on the talents he had. Did she know him at all?

They ate supper and went to bed that evening without speaking. They lay in the king-size Sears Roebuck bed as far apart as possible.

At least the bed was comfortable. With a decent spread on it - maybe something Moroccan instead of this lousy chenille - it would be all right.

Since he didn't have to spend so much time on furniture for the new place, Guido had more time for work. He hoped that in ninety days he could come up with the money. Maybe he would have. But the baby came down with a bad throat. It turned out to be strep. More bills arrived. Doctors had to be paid and expensive antibiotics had to be purchased. And there were too many nights with no sleep.

Guido went to Sears and asked for an extension. They told him interest would start on the ninetieth day at eighteen per cent. He went to the bank and asked if they would add one thousand (he had two hundred) to the mortgage to get him out of difficulty. He found out that banks are bloodless monsters. If you have money, they are eager to loan you what you don't need. If you need money, they consider you a bad risk - and a second-class citizen.

Luciana said: "Okay. I got us into this. I'll get us out."

It was the eighty-eighth day. She took a bus to Boston and came back at five-thirty. "Here it is," she said, and put one thousand dollars in tens and twenties and fifties into Guido's hands.

"Where did you get this?" he asked.

"From Joe Bandi, my cousin."

"Is he the one with fingers missing on one hand?"

"Does it matter?"

"What will this cost?"

"Twenty a week."

"Twenty a week until when?"

"I don't know."

"You mean twenty a week is just interest?"

"All he said was 'Twenty a week.'"

"Luciana, is Joe Bandi a loan shark?"

"How do I know what he is? I told him we needed a thousand. He said: 'Anything you you want, Baby.' Then he peeled off all those bills. 'Twenty a week,' he said. And that was it."

Guido could feel anger rising within him. "If twenty a week is just interest," he said, "then we will be paying over one thousand per cent interest on this money. That's fifty times as much as Sears wanted and that was already outrageous. Don't you understand anything?"

"So after I went all the way to Boston and got you the money, now you can only find fault." She began to cry. "You don't think I can do anything right, do you?"

How could he answer her? When it came to money, she was hopeless. But her tears, and the way he seemed to be the only one to make her aware of her inadequacies, tore him apart.

"*Luciana cara*," he said, and took her in his arms, "*non ti preoccupare*...don't worry. I'll straighten it out. I'll go up to Boston tomorrow and see if there's a way to get this settled."

He lost another day. He drove the truck to Boston. Two or three thousand miles more and a transmission job would be unavoidable. How much would that cost?

He found Joe Bandi in a variety store on Maverick Street. They sold milk and cigarettes and candy. There were a few cans of soup on a shelf. Potato chips. A rack next to the cooler had apples and grapes on it. There were three men in the store. One of them was Joe. Voices came from a back room.

"I'm Guido Bussatti."

"Yeah. I remember. I was to the wedding. Seen the wife just yesterday."

"That's why I'm here. I need to talk to you."

"Talk is cheap. Watch wanna talk about?" The other two men were listening. Joe didn't seem to mind.

"Luciana borrowed a thousand from you yesterday. You told her the payments would be twenty dollars a week."

"That's correct."

"Is that principal or interest?"

"Now wadda you think?"

"I suspect it is interest."

"You right again. Very smart."

"Mr. Bandi, there has been a mistake. I am going to give you back the thousand right now and that will be the end of our business with you."

"Only one thing wrong with what you say." Joe put a three-finger hand on Guido's arm. "There's a penalty for pre-payment. Just like at the bank. Fifty dollars."

Guido pulled his arm free. "That's ridiculous," he said.

Joe smiled. It was not a nice smile. "Better speak pretty to me, Cuz." The other two men in the room had moved one step closer.

Guido drew a long slow breath. This was not a moment in which to lose his temper. "Since we are related, Mr. Bandi," he said, "and because I value your good will, perhaps you will consider reducing the amount of the penalty."

Bandi nodded slightly. "Well," he said, "that's a very high class way to say Gimme a break. I gotta remember that. So we'll call it thirty."

"Twenty - please?"

"Don' push me. You don' know how lucky you are."

So Guido counted out the original thousand and added thirty. He wondered if he should ask for a receipt, then decided to say nothing.

Bandi made a mock bow. "A pleasure to do business with such a genalman," he said. "Remember me, Guido Bussatti, if you are ever in need again."

"I'll do that," Guido said, and left. Never would he forget this maggot. He hoped only that he would never see him again.

From the variety store, so-called, he drove to Don Tito's office. He had to park several blocks farther on in that crowded section and walk back. Don Tito was not there.

An old man, his dry skin all blotchy with brown spots and others that were white where pigmentation had gone awry, sat where Don Tito had always sat. A younger man stood just inside the door.

"Is Don Tito not around?" Guido asked.

"Who is it wants to know?"

"I'm Guido Bussatti. Don Tito is my wife's grandfather and my friend."

"I thought I had seen you," the old man said. "You live now on Cape Cod. No?"

"Yes."

"Don Tito is in the hospital. In a coma. He had a stroke. He don' know nobody. He's just a thing now with tubes an' pumps. Pitiful to see."

The news was a blow to Guido. Don Tito had seemed a center around which all else revolved in this part of his life. Whatever it was he had done here, he had done it as well as it could be done. He had been respected. To Guido he had been a surrogate father, wise and generous. In the envelope Don Tito had given him after the wedding had been five hundred dollars. No strings attached. It had made a vast difference that first year.

Involuntarily, Guido made the sign of the cross. He turned to look through the upper part of the window where a corner of sky could be seen.

"Don Tito spoke of you," said the man who sat in his place. "He said he was happy you got out of the city."

"I would like to see him," Guido said.

"No, you would not. Better you remember him as you knew him. He is gone. That thing in the hospital is not Don Tito. It should be put underground decently, not kept on display."

There was anger in his voice. Guido turned back to him. The old man, too, would not long be a stranger to death. Perhaps he was right. It would be better not to try to see Don Tito.

"*Ha raggione*," he said from the doorway... "you are right. *Grazie. Addio.*"

He walked slowly to his truck, the truck Cardullo had given

him. Cardullo always had cash on him. Was there anyone else he could approach for a loan?

The trucking company office was in the North End too. There was room to park there. "Company cars only," a sign read. "Others will be towed." Did he dare park? Why not?

Cardullo was in the office. When Guido entered he did not get up from the swivel chair in which he was seated. He looked at Guido with no sign of emotion.

"Only one thing could bring you here," he said. "You need money."

What Guido would not have given to be able to deny it! He bowed his head. "I'm sorry. It's only for a short while. Six months. Maybe less. I would not have come except that it is urgent."

"How much?"

Guido raised his eyes to meet those of his father-in-law. "One thousand dollars," he said.

Cardullo let the sound of all those dollars roll away into the corridor behind him. Then he snorted.

"Yesterday Luciana comes to town. She doesn't even come to see her old father and mother. She goes to that shit-eater, Bandi, *merdaiolo*. She gets one thousand from him. What happened to that money?"

So he knew. The word traveled fast. "I gave it back to him twenty minutes ago," Guido said.

"Plus how much?"

"He wanted fifty. He settled for thirty."

"A dollar an hour, eh? I should go kick thirty teeth out of his rotten skull. You heard about Don Tito."

Did he know that Guido had just come from Don Tito's office?

"I heard only minutes ago. Is he really unable to recognize anyone?"

"There is no mind in his body now. What did Luciana do that

she came to Bandi for a thousand dollars?"

"She bought some things for our new home."

"Some things! Some things of one thousand dollars?"

"A little more."

"An' you can't pay for them."

"I was not prepared for this expense."

"I gotta tell you something, Guido Bussatti. Women don' unnerstan money. You the husband. You give the wife twenny-five dollars a week to run the house. Maybe thirty, now you got the baby. Not a penny more. You unnerstan?"

"It would work better that way."

"So make it that way. Sometimes you gotta slap them aroun'." He paused. "You ever laid hands on Luciana?"

"I don't think I could ever hurt her," Guido said. "She made me angry this time, but I love her. I could never harm her."

Cardullo was caught in the middle by his own impulses. If he thought Guido would strike his daughter, who knows what he would do to Guido. But if Guido was not man enough to control his own wife, who could have respect for him?

Guido sensed this. His humiliation was acute.

Cardullo pressed a buzzer on his desk and a young woman came in almost immediately.

"Write a check for one thousand dollars," he ordered, "payable to Guido Bussatti (double ess, double tee). Make it 'as per invoice.' Then make out a bill for one thousand for 'office remodeling' and bring both to me."

She left. "This is a no-interest loan, Guido, but no hurry to repay. With a phony bill for remodeling I save about four hundred dollars on taxes. That makes us even. Maybe I come out ahead." He almost smiled. Then he added: "Here, take this thirty too," and he pulled three tens off a thick roll that had been in his pocket. "I'll go to see Bandi later today. That'll be a little fun before supper."

The ride back to the Cape seemed extra long. Cardullo could have been a lot less decent, but the fact remained that Guido had gone to him on his knees, was in debt to him, would be looked down upon henceforth.

When he got home he told Luciana everything he had done.

"I'm sorry, Guido. Can you forgive me?"

"It's all right," he told her. "I'll go to Hyannis and settle this bill for the furniture this afternoon. Then we'll have to figure a way to make regular payments to your father. That is very important to me."

"I could take a job as a waitress," Luciana said. "I did that once for three weeks. Before I knew you."

"But while you would be out, I would have to stay home with the baby."

"You'd be home anyway. Most waitress jobs are from five to ten. It's evening work."

"I don't like the idea, Luciana. And many nights I have to work."

"Not all nights. Week-ends are are the big nights for waitressing. Maybe I could work just three nights a week."

"And have all kinds of rich men making passes at you."

"So they make a pass. I'm used to that."

"And you smile at them."

"A smile does no harm and it makes for big tips. Look, I need to get out of the house sometimes. And for you, it would mean more time to get to know Pierino. He hardly ever sees you. A boy should know his father."

There was truth enough in that. Pierino was walking now and beginning to talk. He had lost his butterball baby roundness and was getting longer. Mobile features already expressed swift changes of mood. It would be a joy to spend more time with him.

So Guido relented. "Okay," he said. "If you can find a job three nights a week it will be a big help. There's always work around the house for me. I'll keep busy."

Luciana went to work Friday, Saturday and Sunday nights. She landed the job so quickly that Guido suspected she had lined it up even before she spoke of it to him. The restaurant was within walking distance, but usually she took the truck in order not to come home alone after dark, or to avoid being out in bad weather.

What she earned, varied. Guido seldom had any idea how much it was. She spent it as fast as she made it. But each month one hundred dollars went to Cardullo to reduce that debt even if all of it had to come from what Guido was earning.

Luciana was good at remembering orders. She never had to write them down. And with her swinging hips and rippling breasts she was very popular with the old geezers and would-be lechers whose wives looked on with envy at times, with gratitude at others when their old man had something reawakened that would require attention later in the evening.

She liked kidding with the customers. She got all kinds of goodies to eat. She made a lot more money than she admitted. And another waitress there became her friend.

Polly had none of the pectoral embellishment that made Luciana so alluring. She was thin, acerbic in manner, but there was an agressive sexuality about her. Behind her heavy-lidded obsidian eyes lurked a promise of appetites that made men's mouths pucker.

Many nights, after work, if Polly didn't have a date, she and

Luciana would sit in the truck, or in Polly's little VW, talking until midnight, or even later. Guido would be asleep hours before Luciana came home.

Those nights, alone with his small son, were a source of great contentment for Guido. They ate together at the kitchen table, soup and sandwiches, a cookie, milk. If Pierino rubbed honey in his hair to see what his father would do, Guido would put a finger into the sticky tangle and then lick it and pretend it was better than ever - an excellent recipe. And Pierino would try it until he got some hairs in his mouth, which made him decide it was not such a good recipe after all.

They laughed together a great deal and they talked. A lot of it was clowning, making up words and saying things that were nonsense.

When they were through eating, Guido would clean up. Pierino was big enough to carry things from the table to his father at the sink.

They might play for a while later. Guido had collected dozens of small pieces of wood, all sanded and smooth, so they built towers and forts and tunnels on the kitchen floor or in Pierino's room.

At six-thirty they went into the bathroom and Pierino had his bath - another chance to have fun, splashing and laughing.

The little boy had learned how to stand up and pee like a man. His aim was not always accurate but it was improving. He stood on a small platform Guido had made for him that put the bowl at the appropriate height.

Then, when Pierino was in bed, Guido always told him a story. The stories were about animals mostly - raccoons that came in the night and opened the trash barrels, scattering garbage all over the yard, squirrels that stole cookies off the window sill. But sometimes Guido would talk to his son about what it was like when he was little in Castiglion Fiorentino, and in Pierino's mind ancient battlements and immense villas loomed, filled with mystery and magic, while in Guido's memory the ghosts of childhood beckoned, then whispering withdrew.

Those nights, after Pierino was asleep, Guido always found cleaning to do. Luciana grew sloppier by the week when it came to housekeeping. *Cialtrona*, they would have called her in Italy, but this home was so easy to keep gleaming that Guido didn't mind very much. All those formica surfaces in the kitchen, the rubber tiles on the kitchen floor, the ceramic tile in the bathroom - it only took seconds to wipe them clean. Dirty clothes went into the washer. There was almost no dust in this tight house. And the *aspirapolvere*, that miraculous American invention, the vacuum cleaner, sucked away the dirt faster than you could give a shake to a rug.

Guido had to wonder what his father would have said to see him cleaning house. That was woman's work in Italy. Wasn't it here too? Maybe not.

When Luciana first started working, Guido waited up for her, hoping she would not be too tired to make love when she came home. Soon he got used to going to sleep before she returned. Up at five in the morning, he could not keep himself awake much after ten in the evening.

There had been a cooling off, after Pierino was born. She practiced rhythm and avoided all contact for too many days in the middle of the month. Guido wouldn't have minded having a second child. An only child is a lonely child, someone had told him.

Luciana said she wanted to wait. So when he lay next to her in the big bed, all the ripeness of her body close beside him, his desire was greater than ever. When she refused, he did not insist, but his need became ache and resentment. He loved her totally, felt his reponsibility for her and for her happiness, but he wanted her so much that some days he could scarcely concentrate on his work.

One evening, looking for a new bar of soap in the bathroom

cabinet, he came across a kind of latex disk in a small box. He'd never seen anything like it before and it took him a while to realize it was a diaphragm. How long had she had that? Didn't the church say that it was forbidden? And why did she say she depended upon the rhythm method if she used a diaphragm anyway? He never asked her about it, but he felt something had been taken away from him.

Polly came by to get Luciana on their way to work together one afternoon. Guido came home and found the two women at the kitchen table, talking.

"This is my husband," Luciana announced, introducing him. Guido was in work clothes, sawdust in his thick hair, old boots on. Polly was wearing a short skirt and sat with her legs crossed. She didn't get up. "Luciana talks about you all the time," she said.

"She's spoken of you too, to me," Guido replied. Actually, she had said very little about her friend. He had wondered why. Now he had an inkling of what the reason might be. This woman had the look of a predator, a raptor. She gazed at him from under reptilian lids, measuring his weaknesses, it seemed, spotting the cracks in his armor. Luciana could not have spoken about this side of her friend, yet she must have been fascinated by it.

"There's left-over chicken in the fridge and some purée for Pierino. Ice cream too," Luciana said.

"Where is Pierino?"

"He's sleeping. He was out in the yard all afternoon."

"Then he'll never go to sleep tonight. I'll go wake him up."

"And we better get going."

"Nice to have met you," Polly said.

"Come again," Guido answered, then almost wished he hadn't said it. He didn't like her. But maybe it was just a touch of jealousy that made him feel that way. Perhaps he should be glad that Luciana at last had another woman to talk to and be with. No doubt she had been lonely a lot of the time since they came to the

Cape.

Pierino was cranky that evening. His routine had been broken. Luciana should have known better than to let him play through his nap time and then sleep when he always played. He didn't like the purée that was supposed to be his supper. He threw most of it on the floor. Then he was hungry.

Guido, too, was in a bad mood for some reason. He couldn't get over the uneasy feeling that Luciana had teamed up with her friend on an opposite side from his. She was easing away from him. The male/female thing that had brought them together so irresistibly had become a line separating them, men on one side and women on the other.

Almost a year passed before the debt to Cardullo was liquidated. With that out of the way, Guido hoped to have a little extra money at last, but it was just then that the owner of the building where he had his shop told him that if he wanted his lease renewed the rent would increase by a little over one hundred a month.

Guido looked everywhere and discovered that for the location he had he couldn't do better, even at the increased rent. He was not using the upstairs where he and Luciana had lived their second year together and he thought he might sub-let that for the extra money. He even found a young fisherman who wanted it. But the landlord got wind of this. And he knew the fisherman.

"You'd be lucky to get the second month's rent from him," he told Guido. "The guy's a dead beat. He's not even a good fisherman. Anyway, I don't want any sub-lets. Too much can go wrong. There'd be too much wear and tear."

So Guido began using the upstairs for storage space, in the back, and an extra showroom, in the front. He was busy the year 'round. His signs were in demand and many of the so-called antique dealers - some who dealt in genuine antiques, too - had found that he did first-class work at reasonable prices. Maybe if he raised his prices just a little...

Guido enjoyed his work. He knew he was good at it. The long hours didn't upset him. The problem was that he couldn't seem to get ahead.

Luciana began to nag him about never going anyplace, never

entertaining, not having an automobile - "just that old truck."

The truck had held up valiantly. It was battered and rusted, but the motor was still good.

"I'll get a car of my own," Luciana said.

"Have you saved enough money for that?" Guido asked.

"And then some."

"You could have told me."

She was still waitressing. She bought all her own clothes. She still charged things and the bills came to Guido. He complained when it happened.

"I need something for going shopping," Luciana said. "I'd like to get out of this dinky village sometimes. Pierino will be going to nursery school soon and I'll have to get him there, too. I'll buy a car of my own."

Could he stop her? If she had her own car she might calm down and be happier. He felt guilty, as if he had failed her. She had expected more of him. By his standards, they had a great deal. In Italy they would have been considered most fortunate. Here, somehow, there was always something more to be desired. If you couldn't have it, you felt diminished - at least Luciana did.

She bought a Plymouth that was six years old. It was an authentic, state-of-the-art lemon. If it ran for ten days without needing the replacement of some part, it was a wonder. Every couple of weeks Guido had to close the shop for an hour and go and tow her to a service station. Then, as often as not, he'd be the one to get stuck for the repairs.

Luciana was a terrible driver - never signaled her turns, couldn't learn how to park. Guido held his breath when she was out with Pierino.

Where did she go? What did she do? It seemed that she spent most of her time in shopping centers. She came home with things she didn't need and that got lost or discarded before they were used. When Pierino was with her she kept him happy with candy and ice cream. Her idea of a meal was a hot dog and a sundae - for a bonus, she had nothing to clean up. Guido began to get an idea of how much money she made by the amounts that she squandered week after week that she hadn't received from him.

A few times, as gently as he could, he tried to speak to her about money and how to manage it. She only got angry, accusing him of never letting her do anything her own way.

Yet he adored her. He believed she was the most beautiful of all women. Asleep, in the same bed with her, he dreamed of her. At work, the thought of her would make him forget where he was and what he was doing. He wondered if other men loved in the same obsessional manner.

She had begun to treat him as someone, in certain ways, beneath her. He was there to serve her and it seemed he didn't serve her well. It didn't make any difference to him. He worshiped her. When she allowed him to come to her, all else paled.

One afternoon, when Paolino was almost seven, Polly came to the shop. It was July, a sweltering summer afternoon when everyone had gone to the beach. Guido had a sign that was due for delivery. The carving had not gone well and had taken too long. He was sweaty and dirty and the final coat of paint for the border had filled the shop with fumes that made him dizzy even with all doors and windows open.

Polly was wearing a simple white dress, straps at the shoulders, a black border at her knees.

"So this is where you spend all your days," she said.

He hadn't seen her for several weeks. She and Luciana were both working at another restaurant that summer but were as close as ever. Usually Luciana drove to Polly's in the late afternoon so they could go to work together.

"This would be a good day not to be here," Guido said.

The heat did not seem to affect Polly. Her skin was dry. "Show me around," she said.

He gave her the guided tour - the table bench, the band saws, the lathe, some finished signs, his sets of chisels, drawings, layouts.

Her eyes were on him, not on the things he pointed out. He couldn't tell about her, if she was really absorbing everything, or if she didn't care at all. She didn't comment on anything he said. Was she more communicative with Luciana? She must have been.

"And what's upstairs?" she asked.

He led her up the steep flight of stairs to his showroom where he kept a few of the valuable antiques he was restoring, along with some wood sculpture which no one had bought so far, but which he felt compelled to make from time to time.

"And this is just a storeroom," Guido said, stepping into the back room, which was piled high with different kinds of wood on racks, and broken things that would be repaired in time, or used in one way or another.

He turned to go back out but she blocked his way. She put both hands on his shoulders. "Now," she said. Nothing else.

And he knew, for sure, what he had known from the minute she walked in downstairs, that this was why she had come and that she knew he would be a party to it, without hesitation.

If anyone entered the shop, they would know.

Her hands went to his waist and undid the clasp on his belt. He still wore a pair of corduroy pants he had brought with him from Italy, buttons on the fly, the knees patched, cuffs frayed.

She unbuttoned his fly, put her hands on his sweaty flanks inside his shorts, pushed down so pants and underwear fell to the floor. She lifted her dress up under her arms. She had nothing on under the opaque cotton.

He stared at her flat belly, yellow-brown in the semi-darkness of the storeroom, the heavy labia, low between her legs. She brought one hand to her mouth and wet the palm with her tongue then lowered it, transferring saliva to him, caresssing him for a moment before guiding him in.

She leaned back onto a bureau behind her, balanced on the end of her spine. She clasped his shoulder blades with both hands, lifted her legs off the floor, spreading them, digging her heels into the lower part of his back.

He lurched against her, humping her, whacking his loins against her hard pelvis, thrusting and coming to climax before he even realized what was happening.

Did it take five minutes? Even less? She was gone. She hadn't spoken again.

He was aware of the smell of sweat and saliva and semen mixed with another odor that belonged to the woman. It was on him, all over him.

He picked up his shorts and pants and stepped into the bathroom and stripped and took a hot shower. But when he was dressed again he could still smell it, or thought that he could, a faint clinging sharp stink of corruption.

And when he reached for the light switch, he noticed his hand shook, that hand which ordinarily was so steady it could draw a line as straight as a ruler, the same hand that had gripped Polly's hard buttocks and pulled.

A vision of two dogs going at it in the street flickered in his head. That's what it had been like, an animal act, a wordless violent struggle, over as fast as it started, meaningless - or was it? What did it do to his relationship with Luciana? If it meant nothing, then why did he feel that something fundamental had shifted position in his life?

He had never been unfaithful before. Even when he was half out of his mind with desire for Luciana and she turned away from him, he didn't think of other women. Was gratification this simple? This available? How many other women might he have as easily? He hadn't even gone looking. Suppose he started seeking others?

But he didn't want to. It was still Luciana he loved. He couldn't imagine loving anyone else, although now he could imagine finding release elsewhere.

So then was sex like a bodily function, like taking a leak, a thing you had to do, then forgot? He couldn't accept that. Love and intimacy were part of something bigger when the two were joined. Sex, without love, was even less than love, without sex.

He needed some time by himself. The thought of facing Luciana and Pierino at this moment was intolerable.

He phoned Luciana and said he had to go into Sandwich on some work to be estimated. He'd be home rather late. He'd grab a bite to eat out, someplace.

After closing the shop he drove to Sandwich. He ate fried flounder and coleslaw at a roadside stand and then went on to the marina on the Canal.

He parked and started walking. It would be cooler in a while when the sun went down. A light breeze had come up even now.

Boats were coming in - a dragger, a couple of smaller craft. The men on the two private boats were calling to each other, trying to find out how the other had made out. Fishermen - what evasions were they not capable of! Guido was beginning to understand their ways. He'd listened to them often enough. If they had a successful day, they'd do anything to hide the fact. If they'd found a hot spot, they'd rather come up empty than lead someone else to it. If the lure they were using, or the type of bait they had on, was working, they'd haul their fish on the side of the boat away from the eyes of anyone else around. They'd even drop a fish rather than let a competitor see what rig the fish were hitting.

Gulls and terns filled the air to the stern of the dragger. Someone aboard was shucking scallops and the birds were in a frenzy to scavenge whatever was chucked overboard.

Guido walked out the path to the jetty. People were picking blueberries there, highbush blueberries that would be made into pies and cobblers and breakfasts with fresh cream and sugar on them.

The jetty, huge irregular boulders, battered by countless storms, treacherous, covered with weeds and slime, extended far out into the mouth of the canal. He made his way to the end and stood there in the cleansing air of the late afternoon.

A man with a spinning reel was casting in the direction of the black can in the channel, a surface plug on his line, a popper. He was intent on what he was doing, didn't turn to acknowledge Guido's presence, but knew he was there.

Guido watched. He hadn't tried this kind of fishing yet. He kept telling himself he would. He'd been out in the Bay a couple of times in a twenty-two foot boat with a customer whose only passion was fishing. It seemed all native Cape Codders were fisherman - the men that is. Some found the way to go fishing every month of the year. They lived in their trucks and their wagons. When, for some reason they couldn't get out, they stayed home and worked on their gear. Did they have wives? Couldn't they stand them?

Wasn't he away from home as much as any fisherman, though? But God knows it wasn't because he wanted to avoid his family. Except right now. That was the case, wasn't it? He was staying away because he had done something he couldn't face up to. He felt guilty. Was guilty. Could there be any justification? If a man is denied something he needs, can he be blamed for accepting it when offered, if the source is tainted?

- You're just looking for excuses, he told himself.

A thought surfaced in him and he wanted to turn his back on it, but it pursued him. Luciana stayed away from home too, as much as she could. What was her reason?

No. It couldn't be. It was ignoble of him to think it, even for a second.

Yet he knew his marriage was in trouble. This thing that had happened to him, that he had let happen, would have been impossible their first years together. What had changed? What had allowed it? Did marriages go through stages, as children do, growing up? Certainly the initial excitment, the anticipation of and the reveling in physical love that marked the beginning could not be maintained indefinitely. There had to come a time when what had been new or unknown became familiar and routine. When you know everything there is to know about your partner, doesn't some of the zest go out of the relationship?

So the luster was gone. That didn't have to mean it was over. The tenderness he felt for Luciana was in no way diminished. And the way he loved Pierino made tears come to his eyes.

His son was seven already. He was learning to swim this summer, was like a dolphin in the water. Luciana, who had never learned to swim, had kept him from learning sooner. This year Pierino had defied her and in no time he was diving and even swimming underwater.

The Bay water was terribly cold, but in Barnstable Harbor, when the tide turned and flowed back out of the marsh, the water was warm enough even for Guido.

Shifting sand bars and flats made it a great place to wander as the tide ebbed. Pierino knew the names of all the local shellfish already. He had collected eels, too, and horseshoe crabs and red crabs and spike mackerel trapped in pools at the bottom of the tide.

The boy was quick to learn. He spoke English perfectly, was already a reader. Too bad he wasn't learning any Italian. Luciana discouraged it. This troubled Guido. The Italian Guido spoke was not just some dialect, like that of so many other Italians in America, including Luciana's Sicilian family. Guido spoke what was considered the purest Italian. A pity his son would not be learning from him. He would have picked it up naturally in no time, Guido was sure.

A dark bird with the wings of a falcon came over the water toward him. It was flying fast. White spots showed in its wings. A tern with a sand eel in its bill suddenly went into almost vertical flight and the black marauder passed only inches under it, then wheeled, changing course, defying the laws of momentum, and rose in pursuit of the tern. The tern, graceful and swift, was no match for the jaeger. It dropped the sand eel from its bill and the other, banking and swooping, caught the snack in mid-air before it had fallen five feet, then sailed off into the ruby glow of the horizon.

It was time to head back. The water had risen and some of the jetty was covered. Guido came close to slipping on wet rocks. The water there was cold and the current fast. Not a few men have fallen into the Canal and gone for a chill swim. Some have been carried out into the Bay and have not returned.

By the time Pierino - they called him Peter then - was in High School, Guido's marriage had all but ended. Luciana no longer slept in the same bed with him. She kept their big bedroom for herself and he had been relegated to a cot in the small room that had been Pierino's - Peter's.

Peter had taken over the guest bedroom. He was a stocky sullen adolescent who worked out with weights at the gym and played center on the varsity football team.

Luciana had stopped working as a waitress. She still had her own car, a second-hand Rambler, and summers she worked in a department store in Hyannis. She knew a lot of people. Guido had met a few of them - a buyer for Filene's, a hairdresser who had her own shop and was doing very well, a woman who said she was a singer - all, decidedly pushy types, women who used men only to get what they wanted and who seemed cold and barren to Guido.

He and Luciana kept different hours. She slept late into the morning and was usually out until midnight. He continued to rise at five and fix his own breakfast in order to get to his shop a little after six. They did not even meet at suppertime very often. She'd be gone by then, leaving something to warm up, or word to go in town and buy a take-out meal.

Father and son sat on opposite sides of the kitchen table and had long since stopped talking about anything of importance. Guido would look at his son and see a young man he didn't know at all, one who had grown up under his mother's wing, who'd accepted her judgement that Guido was never going to amount to anything.

The boy had seemed to be waiting for something for several years and it turned out to be football. Guido went to the games in which Peter played and tried to understand what was going on, but the role of the center eluded him. He wished Peter had taken up soccer. That was a sport he understood. Peter was a natural athlete - swimmer, runner. He could have played center forward in soccer and been outstanding. They would have had something to share. But football was pretty much the American sport, according to Peter. Not soccer. That was a game for 'Guineas and Spics.'

When Peter said that to him, Guido almost lost control. "What are you saying?" he asked. "Aren't we 'Guineas?' Where did you get this way of speaking about Italians and Spanish-speaking people? Is there something wrong with coming from another background?"

Luciana was with them that evening. Mother and son had looked at each other and in their eyes was confirmation of what Guido had just suggested. These two did think there were lower class people, by birth, and they wanted to disassociate themselves. Was there any sense in that? Guido was hurt and perplexed. Certainly he felt no shame about being Italian.

At the shop, Guido continued to work long hours. As costs had risen, he had raised prices. More and more people kept moving to the Cape and demand for his services increased so that he could have put in twenty hours a day from one end of the year to the other.

Fortunately, in his work he found genuine satisfaction. He did not think of himself as a artist, but rather as an artisan. What he did was creative and original. To take materials into your own hands and transform them into something tangible and graceful and enduring, is this not one of the most gratifying activities in which a man may be engaged?

He thought sometimes of those clerks in the supermarkets, those tellers in banks, those men on production lines - they did useful work, admittedly, but it was mechanical, repetitious, uncreative. In the long run it would become deadly, at least it would have become deadly for him. He would never have been able to keep going, as he had, in any other line of work.

He made enough money to keep his family together, to pay the bills, to give Luciana most of what she demanded. He'd never be rich. He'd never really expected he would be. But his work filled his days - long days from sun-up to sunset - and a sense of accomplishment lived with him.

But two months later he wrote home:

"*Carissimi, ho da dirvi una cosa poco piacevole*...Dearest Ones, I have something not pleasant to tell you. My wife, Luciana, has divorced me. Before God, we are still married, but in the eyes of the law, here, we are no longer man and wife.

"Luciana hired a lawyer and I was charged with 'extreme mental cruelty.'

"You should understand that here this is more or less a formula for obtaining divorce. By no stretch of the imagination could it be said that I was ever cruel to Luciana, unless to love someone who no longer cares for you is a form of mental cruelty. I wouldn't know about that.

"I am not trying to say that I am blameless. What happened to our marriage was undoubtedly as much my doing as Luciana's. I have thought, sometimes, that Luciana was too young to get married when she did. She had no way of knowing what marriage entailed. Neither did I. Maybe we should have waited. Be that as it may, once married, it was up to us to make the best of it. And for a time we did.

"Luciana's haste to get married had something to do with her impatience with her family and her immigrant Italian surroundings.

"This is a hard thing to explain to you. We are very class conscious in Italy, but we are all Italians. In America, though, there is a stereotype of the Italian immigrant. He is fat and greasy. He has a pushcart or a hurdy-gurdy. He murders the English language when he speaks. He lives on *spaghetti* and *vino*. He was a bootlegger during Prohibition and nowadays he is involved in gambling, vice, drugs - they like to talk about the *mafia* here. So there is a real stigma attached to being Italian. Luciana wanted to escape from this stigma. She made the mistake of marrying an Italian.

"We left the neighborhood where she grew up. We left her family and relatives, some of whom have been deeply hurt by the fact that we have almost never been back. We came to a place full of old Yankees, New Englanders from way back. (Well, way back in this country means only a couple of hundred years - about the time our building in Castiglione was getting its second roof.)

"Anyway, we put a distance between ourselves and the environment of Luciana's youth. But we brought a lot of Italy with us. In me. I cannot be anything but proud of a heritage that goes back to the Romans and Etruscans, that includes men like Leonardo and Masaccio and Dante and Piero della Francesca, Bruneleschi, Vivaldi, Michelangelo - a list as long as the road from here to Arezzo - all the way down to Moravia and Italo Calvino and Rosai. (Did I tell you that Attilio has a Rosai in his apartment in New York?)

"Luciana found that the man she loved - for a while - and married, was the embodiment of much from which she had wanted to flee. It confused her. I think this is one of the sources of our trouble. Maybe, if I had gone into contracting and had built a lot of cheap houses and made 'big bucks,' as they say here, or if I had started a factory and cranked out thousands of plaster figurines - what these people call 'lawn sculpture' - then the money would have been enough to save our marriage. Money, here, as in Italy, makes even the most ignorant person revered. I don't know.

"I have a craft. I work with wood, as you do, Papà, and I do good work. I take pride in what I do. But this is another face of the stereotype of the small-time Italian immigrant - shopkeeper, shoemaker, sign painter. Do you see?

"You have begun to receive some of the sculpture I make. These pieces are not sought for yet. Perhaps they never will be. But I hope to have a little gallery in Italy, someday. Store what I send you in a safe place, please.

"The divorce decree assigned our home to Luciana, but I must continue to make the payments on the mortgage until such time as she sells the house or the mortgage is paid off. The court gave Luciana custody of Pierino - whom she insists on calling Peter. He's already seventeen so that doesn't mean much. The sad part is that long ago he lost interest in me. As he takes on the responsibilities of a man there is a chance that he will turn to me again. It's something to keep me from despair.

"You will never know with how much longing I think of you, Minca, Piero, Franca. Someday I will return to Castiglion Fiorentino. I will not come empty-handed. You'll see.

"*Un abbraccione. Guido.*"

He deliberately avoided telling them how the lawyer had maligned him in court.

"This man, from the beginning, has failed to support his family adequately. For the first year of married life he forced his young bride, then only eighteen, to live in a barn. Before long, because her husband could not even afford to furnish their only real home, she was compelled to seek work as a waitress. As if poverty were not enough, my client was also subjected to the extreme humiliation caused by her husband's adulterous relationship with her closest friend."

Should he have allowed the diatribe to continue without protest? To be sure, Polly had returned a half dozen times and Guido had almost welcomed the brutal mindless coupling that followed. He wondered, though, if the two women had planned it from the start. Was entrapment in Luciana's mind? If she hated him that much what difference did it make what anyone thought?

As for the lawyer, he was someone who filled Guido with loathing. For a fee he'd say anything. Had he been hired by Guido, he would have taken the opposite side without question. Maybe Guido should have hired him since, in the end, he was ordered to pay his fee.

Guido cleared a part of the storeroom, the part that had once been his and Luciana's bedroom, and fixed a corner there where he slept and cooked for himself. He worked longer hours than ever. Support payments for Pierino were to terminate when the boy reached eighteen years of age, but when he required knee surgery his senior year in High School, after a football injury that ended his chances for a professional career, the bills were forwarded to Guido and it took him three years to pay off that debt.

The rent for his shop and so-called apartment increased every time he seemed about to get ahead, but the location was excellent and he couldn't afford to move.

Sundays he didn't work. For a long time he had. Then he had decided he needed one day off each week. What was the purpose in pushing himself to a point at which no day was ever any different from the others?

He began going to church on Sundays. It was pleasant to let himself think there might be a God after all. He went to St. Mary's which wasn't a Catholic church, but was close to it. He felt no need to go to confession. What was there to confess? Those trivial peccadilloes he had been taught were sinful had long since ceased to trouble his conscience. He believed that if you were honest in your personal relationships, if you harmed no one knowingly, then little blame could ever fall on you.

At the same time, he had begun to entertain an idea that raised serious questions of wrong-doing and guilt. It was only a whisper somewhere at the back of his mind, a small Devil's voice suggesting he had been given cause. He half heard it. Half listened. At first he rejected it completely, but it wouldn't go away. In church, in the presence of a God in whom he only half believed, he let the idea come part way out of the darkness where it usually hid. Did God, if he existed, know what was in his mind? God was all-knowing, he had been told. If God was all-knowing, yet gave him no sign one way or the other, what did that imply?

Guido hadn't knelt in prayer for years. He felt the urge to do so. In church he could kneel and no one would look askance at him. He knelt and tried to pray but no words came. He let his mind go empty, become a receptor only. He made a conscious effort to listen, to see, to sense whatever message might be there to guide him. If there was any, it failed to reach him.

He got off his knees and sat once more on the ess-curved bench. He looked around. There were twice as many women as men in the church, some older couples, a few families. Mostly, there were ladies over forty and many who were quite elderly.

It came to him with a certain amount of shocked surprise that church, not the night spots and taverns, was the ideal place to pick up a woman.

Sure enough, on going outdoors again, he fell into step with someone who had spotted him in the congregation, a lady of his own age who lived on Rendezvous Lane. She was round and jovial and a brisk walker. It was she who picked him up.

"You're the sign man, aren't you?" she asked.

"I have a shop in the Village, yes. You've seen it then?"

"Passed it many times. I should come in and see some of your work."

"Please do. I'm almost always there."

"Do you live upstairs in the building?"

"I do now. I did for a while about twenty years ago, too, when I was first married."

"Your wife left you?"

"She divorced me."

The lady stopped walking and turned to scrutinize him. "Why would anyone divorce a man like you?" Then she checked herself. "Of course I have no business asking such a thing."

"It's all right," Guido said. "I don't mind talking about it. We were very young when we married. I remember Luciana's mother warning me beforehand that we might grow in different directions. May I ask, have you been married?"

"Can you tell that I no longer am?"

"I think if you were on your way home to a husband we would not be saying the things we are."

"You're right. My husband died."

"I'm sorry you had to suffer."

"There's no need to be sorry. I married a man thirty years older than I. He had a lot of money and he was not very demanding. I married him for his money. You married for love, I imagine. Neither one of us got what we expected."

Was she always this frank, Guido wondered, or was her bluntness a way of covering hurt she did not choose to acknowledge?

"Didn't you at least get the money when he died?"

"It didn't work out that way. He went mental in his last years. If he'd been a poor man, he would have been put away. Instead, his lawyers kept buying his way out of scrapes. He thought he was some kind of G-man and he'd get in his car and race down the highway and make some bewildered motorist pull over. Then he'd tell the fellow he was under arrest for espionage, or drug-dealing. He caused several accidents. There were civil suits and damage suits. After he had a stroke, and died, judgements against his estate took literally everything. I don't even own the house. I can only live in it. I lose even a place to live if I move out."

Her name was Edith. She worked in a dress shop. Her candor appealed to Guido.

He walked her home that day, and the following week too. They began seeing each other every Sunday. The affair was a comfortable one in which neither expected anything momentous.

The house on Rendezvous Lane enjoyed a view of the harbor. It had been built with care, but without maintenance was beginning to look a bit seedy. The owners hoped it would get bad enough so that Edith would move out. Edith couldn't afford repairs, but she couldn't afford to move, either. Shingles were missing already and a shutter had fallen on the street side. The yard was overgrown.

Guido offered to fix some of the things that called for attention. His sense of order was offended by signs of disrepair, but Edith didn't want him to do anything about the external look of the property.

Indoors, she kept the living room, the kitchen, one bath and a study spotless. Her bedroom, also spotless, was on the second floor. It was there that she and Guido made leisurely love. No one ever came to disturb them. They were discrete, but in time the neighbors surely realized they were lovers. It didn't matter to them. The tacky look of the house troubled them much more since it lowered the value of their own homes.

Often, after church, they went for long walks. Sometimes they'd take Guido's truck, a '65 Ford at that time, and drive to Chapin Beach, or Wianno, or Sippewisset and get out and walk there. Both loved the tidelands and beaches of the Cape, the salt air and the changing odors of the marsh - the rank rotting hydrogen sulfide reek of some seasons, the sweet heady fragrance of flowering grasses at others.

They were content with each other. They ate together, those Sundays, sharing expenses. Sometimes Guido would read in the afternoon in the study where Edith's old husband had assembled a first-rate library of American fiction, including mysteries and thrillers that Guido especially liked. Near midnight he would walk back to his own quarters in the Village. The streets were usually completely empty. A drunk, a Barnstable cruiser might be abroad.

That word often came to mind on those evenings. Living in the shadow of the Courthouse, meeting lawyers and court officers from time to time, Guido had learned that there was still a charge on the books in Massachusetts of Being Abroad in the Nighttime. Once in a long while - probably as calculated harassment - some known or suspected miscreant would be picked up on that charge. Guido could have been taken in on it too, had there been any reason.

But everyone knew him. Almost everyone knew his story. He was considered a quiet, perhaps rather ineffectual man who avoided trouble and kept mostly to himself, a foreigner, a hard worker, a fixture readily recognized and therefore nearly invisible.

When Peter got married, he didn't send his father an invitation. Guido only learned of the event months later, by chance, when a client asked if it was his son who had carried off the pretty daughter of a local policeman and moved to another state.

The news was a cruel blow to Guido. He had hoped that with time his son would have a change of heart, that the incomprehensible barrier separating them would come down and they could get to know each other again. It was not to be.

Guido wrote to Pierino, sent him a wedding present - a check for five hundred dollars he could scarecely afford - never had an answer, though the cancelled check came back promptly enough.

Four years later, unable to accept the pain any longer, he took a day off and drove to Waterbury, in Connecticut. His son was athletic coach in a High School there. Guido drove up to the house about noon. He hadn't told anyone he was coming. He rang the bell on a neat suburban bungalow and a young woman with an apron over her dress opened the door.

"I am Peter's father," Guido told her.

The young woman was uncertain what to do or say. "What do you want?" she asked.

"Is my son at home?"

"He's at the school now."

"Perhaps I should go there to find him." It was a suggestion to help her out of her obvious embarrassment.

But she said: "Well, you might miss him that way. He'll be

home within the hour. Is anything wrong?"

"No. I just thought...Peter would not be displeased to see me. It has been a long time since we've seen each other."

She still hesitated. Then she said: "Why don't you come in? I'm Margot. I've often wondered about you."

Guido entered the house and Margot led the way to the kitchen where two small girls were seated at a square table.

"This is Lucy," Margot said. "She's almost four now. And this is Maggie. She's two."

"Who are you?" Lucy asked.

"I am your grandfather," Guido said. "My name is Guido."

Lucy had long straight fair hair. She tipped her head to one side and looked up at him with the one eye that wasn't hidden in that position. "Gooey dough?" She said. "That's a funny name."

"I guess it is, when you think of it that way," Guido said. "It is an Italian name. Names can be quite funny. I once had a cousin from the south of Italy and his name was Baccigalupo."

"Did that mean something?"

"It probably did, but I am not sure what. Maybe it meant 'Kisses from the wolf' because *bacci* means kisses and *lupo* means wolf."

"Do they have wolves in Italy?"

"They used to. Romulus, for whom Rome was named, was suckled by a wolf, according to the legend."

"What is 'suckled?'"

"When Romulus and his brother Remus were hungry, the mother wolf nursed them. They took milk from her."

"You mean like Mommy still nurses Maggie sometimes?"

"Wolves nurse their babies just as human mothers do."

"Do you know lots of stories like that one?"

"Well, not just like that one."

In no time both little girls were perched on his knees. He had not held a small child for ages and ages. It took him back to the time when Pierino was little and a profound closeness existed between them. That time had not lasted long. Ever since then the distance between then had grown greater and greater. He hoped that his coming to Watertown would bring them nearer again.

"Time for your naps," Margot said. "Run along now."

Guido set each child on the floor.

"Will you be here when we get up from our naps?" Lucy asked.

"I'm not sure," Guido said.

Lucy's expression was serious. "Then I better kiss you goodby now," she said.

Guido leaned down and Lucy put her arms around his neck to give him a wet kiss.

"Me too. Me too," said Maggie.

Then Lucy took her sister's hand and led her off to their room, or rooms.

That total trust and love that only a small child can bestow had moved Guido. He was embarrassed to have tears on his face. Margot noticed.

"They're usually very slow to decide they like someone," she said, "but they didn't hesitate with you. You're very good with children."

"Little children are the nicest of all people," Guido said. "Then they grow up..."

"Children are likely to be good judges of character."

Was she saying that especially for his benefit? Guido thought that maybe she wanted him to know her sympathies were with him. "You have not heard too many good things about me, I suppose," he said.

"Peter's mother has come to visit here several times. She bad-mouthed you a lot. I thought it sounded unfair. Now I'm sure."

Margot was rather plain, quite fair, her features on the sharp side. She was not a woman one would notice in a crowd. Her feet were firmly planted on the earth, though. She had a no-nonsense female directness that pleased Guido. Common sense and assurance marked her manner. It had already been communicated to Lucy. If this woman liked him, she would know how to influence Peter.

"Thank you, Margot," Guido said. "And you could call me Guido - or gooey dough, as your daughter thought it sounded."

They both smiled.

"They're delightful little girls. Maybe if Luciana and I had had a daughter, after having Pierino, things would have turned out differently."

"Do you think so?"

"There's no way of telling. I would like to think so. I wish things had not turned out as they have."

They heard the front door open. "That's Peter now," Margot said. "Peter," she called. "Here's a surprise for you. Come see."

Guido got to his feet as his son strode to the kitchen.

The boy, a large man now, two hundred pounds or more, five foot eleven at least, filled the door from the other room.

"Hello, Peter," Guido said.

Peter stopped in his tracks. "What are you doing here? Is something wrong? Is mother all right?"

"Your mother is fine," Guido said. "As far as I know nothing is wrong."

"She's not sick? Nothing's happened to her?"

"I never hear from her, Peter. Her lawyer writes me when he thinks of some new way to get money from me. He doesn't say what she is doing, or if she is well."

"But you know perfectly well how much trouble she's had."

"I'm sorry. I don't know. What trouble?"

"Trying to live on nothing. You were supposed to provide support."

"I was ordered," Guido sighed as he pronounced the word, "to keep up all payments on our home."

"Her home."

"If you wish. I had been led to understand that your mother would live in the house. Instead, she rented it and had all the income and none of the expenses."

"How else could she have supported herself, poor woman?"

"In any case, she had quite a decent rental income for many years and when the mortrgage was all paid off, and at last I was free of that burden, she sold the house and got almost fifty thousand dollars for it."

"And had to pay taxes on that because you were too cheap to take care of them."

"Her astute lawyer attempted to make me pay capital gains on the sale, but at that point I balked, Peter. I realized no capital gains. The house had been a capital drain on me for twenty years. Your mother may have had to pay something like eight thousand dollars in taxes out of an income, that year, of over fifty thousand. The rental income for that year probably covered eighty per cent of the taxes she had to pay. Don't tell me she has already spent or squandered all that money."

"You would put it in those terms - 'squandered.' As if she were a total incompetent. You never respected her, did you?"

"Peter. Peter. Can't we start over? I came here to see you in the hope that we could get to know each other again. I've met my two beautiful grandchildren, your little girls who are irresistible. I've had a chance to talk for a few minutes with Margot, who is a strong remarkable woman. I'm happy to see what a wonderful home and family you have. Can't we be kind to each other?"

Peter just glared at his father. "Kindness is not something I could have learned from you. I wish you had not come here. I hope you won't come again. Now goodbye."

Guido was still standing. His son stepped aside and Guido walked out of the kitchen and through the living room. Margot remained silent and rigid beside the refrigerator.

Guido opened the front door himself and went out and closed it softly behind him. Two teen-agers on bicycles whizzed by. He got into his truck and drove a mile out of town and parked and sat there sobbing, unable to control himself, the ache in him, the hurt, so big he would gladly have died.

That was in 1974. Guido was fifty-one then and what was there to show for all the years he'd been here, all he'd worked for? He wondered, in the evenings when he went upstairs to fix something to eat and then to lie down, was there any point in keeping on? If he packed it all up and went back to Italy at least there would be his mother and father and sister to be with and the awful loneliness would be over.

The affair with Edith was more of an arrangement than anything else. There was little emotional involvement. And they were not seeing as much of each other as they once had.

Guido knew he was letting himself sink into self-pity and that his work was not as careful as it had once been. He wanted to kick himself out of it but seemed to lack the willpower.

Then in the paper one day he saw that a certain 'Flyin' Fingers' was playing in a restaurant in Dennis. He was there three nights a week. Had he been there long? Guido went to hear him the next evening and found him at a baby grand piano in a small bar. It was a Thursday night and there were only a few customers present. Guido got a glass of white wine from the bartender. Then went to stand near the piano. Fingers was playing a song Guido had never heard before.

"What's the name of that piece?" Guido asked, when the music stopped.

"That's called 'Passion Flower.' Johnny Hodges used to play it."

Fingers looked at Guido then. "I know your voice," he said.

"And I remember your face. It was a long time back, though."

Guido was smiling. "I saw your name in a newspaper ad and came over to see you, Mr. Flyin' Fingers."

"Guido. That's it. And the last name...I never used to forget a name."

"It has been a lot of years. Almost thirty now."

"And you remember me?"

"You were the first black man I met in America."

"An' you were on the road. Bummin' rides. Now I got it. Sure." Fingers stood up and they shook hands. He was a little bit stooped now and his full head of hair was pure white. Otherwise, he hadn't change much. "You've stayed here, in the USA, all these years?"

"All these years. Yes. I've never gone back home. But I think I will before much longer."

"What you been doin' all these years?"

"I married, but my wife divorced me. I make signs and restore antiques. I have a shop in Barnstable Village. And you?"

"Still playin' piano. Never got the big break, but never went hungry."

"Your playing is beautiful. I knew it would be."

"Fingers don't fly like they used to. Maybe what they do has more meaning now, though."

They sat together at a corner table when Fingers took a break after nine.

"So you'll be goin' home one of these days." Fingers was hunched forward, head sunk between his big shoulders, crown of white hair alight over his old dark face. "Will it be what you want it to be?" he asked.

"Maybe not," Guido answered. "It will be different. Changed. And I will see it with different eyes."

"World is changin' faster all the time," Fingers said. "We can't hardly keep up with it. I think about goin' home sometimes. Only trouble is, I don't know where home is anymore.

"We lived in Bridgeport when I was little. Six of us. Two boys and four girls. Parents dead a long time, in a accident. We all split up years and years ago. My grandaddy was a slave in Georgia. Was Bridgeport home? Is home in Georgia? Or is home some place on the Gold Coast I never saw, never will see, never heard the name of?

"You lucky, Guido. You have a place to go to that you can call home and not wonder if that's what it is."

"Didn't you ever marry and have a family?"

"Never did. Had lots o' women, both white an' black. Thought about marriage. Always figured it'd come later. Is that what makes a home? Marriage? A wife? Children?"

"It didn't work that way for me," Guido said.

"You have had the music, though," Guido added. "A whole lifetime of making music. That may be better than anything. Music doesn't ever turn against you, does it?"

The telegram came early one morning. He had just opened the shop.

PAPA STA MORENDO. INUTILE VENIRE. SCRIVERO. FRANCA...Father is dying. Useless to come. Will write. Franca.

The letter, three days later, said Piero had suffered a heart attack just after supper. They'd rushed him to the hospital, but there had been no hope of recovery and he had died after two days.

Guido was deeply affected by his father's death. His father had always seemed old to him, but he had always been there. He would die some day, of course, but Guido had never prepared himself for the actual event.

- I will never see him again, he thought. Now I will never have a chance to tell him Goodbye. In all these years I never let him know how much his help and his trust and his love meant to me.

He remembered the smell of the glue pot in his father's shop, the turpentine fumes, the sweet pungent perfume of fresh-worked wood - cedar and cherry and walnut. He was only four or five years old when his father first used to take him to work with him and with infinite patience showed him the tools of his trade and answered every one of his questions.

His father was, had been, a gentle man, a man who had probably never spoken a word in anger in all his life. He worked every day - six days a week in his shop, and after church on Sunday he would be busy in the small plot of land where he raised all their vegetables, had fruit trees, grapes, a few chickens. Wife and daughter and son had never known luxury, but they had never lacked anything essential either. His father had always provided for them.

What would La Minca and Franca do now without all that Piero had always given them? His mother was getting way on in years, too. Her eyesight had failed, he remembered from some letter a couple of years back. She wouldn't be able to earn the money she once had if she could no longer see.

He needed to think seriously about returning to Italy, but he mustn't go back empty-handed. Could he save enough money to make a difference? Now that he didn't have to give anything to Luciana anymore, maybe he could put aside enough each month to set himself up in a small gallery in Arezzo in a year or two. But would that provide an income for three? He could continue the work his father had always done. There were things he had learned in America that might make his work more desirable. Or had he lost touch with some of the old ways so that he would not be as much sought out?

There was the idea he had had about a way to get his hands on a lot of money. It still lurked in the shadows at the back of his mind, a tempter, a way to get even that would provide a *gruzzolo*, an initial stake, which would make everything else easy.

He didn't want to injure anyone, or to run the risk of injuring anyone, physically, but he liked the idea of giving two groups of individuals a taste of their own medicine. It would take meticulous planning. He'd have to be lucky. And patient. Very patient. But if it worked...

His small savings account increased regularly. He set himself a minimum amount that must be added each month. There was purpose, once more, in what he did and he had time to think about the sculpture that he would work on when he had more leisure. He took time to complete at least one work each month and sent it off to Franca for storage until he could get home and open a gallery. The shipping agent said he was foolish to send stuff abroad. "If you can't sell it here, why would anyone buy it in Italy?"

"When rich Americans come to Italy," Guido replied, "they will be told about a famous sculptor who lived for many years in a small village on Cape Cod. My gallery will contain some driftwood and phragmites and a ship model perhaps, Cape Cod nostalgia. They will sense something of home and they will be glad to speak English with a foreign gentleman. When they look on my bizarre sculpture they will be puzzled. They will hesitate. But many will decide to buy. You will see. Well...you won't see, but I may write and tell you."

"I won't live that long," the agent said.

Guido did not think that would have any effect on sales.

He had a panel truck by then. It had heavy duty springs because he sometimes hauled considerable loads of furniture. The sign business was steady, but trade in antiques frequently led to handsome profits. He had developed an eye for valuable items and spent one day a week scouting to find them.

There was a period of a month or more when he wondered if

he even needed to go through with the plan he had. Maybe he was stupid to take a chance on getting caught and going to jail and being disgraced. Wouldn't he have enough money without the extra? He could pack up and go anytime with no risk at all - or no risk except the one of not having enough money to do what he wanted to do in style.

Far bella figura, they said at home, and he wanted that.

He chose a Sunday night in late November. It was windy and quite cold and a flat layer of clouds covered the sky. For several years he had parked his truck in the lot behind the new Registry of Deeds. It was off the street that way at night. A stairway, outdoors, ran down to the parking lot from a fire exit in the Registry. There was no regular patrol of the area. Security was limited. Guido had lived nearby for so long that he knew the habits and routines of all those who might have any reason to be around in the nighttime.

In the Barnstable House of Correction, a severe brick structure on the rise behind the Registry and the Courthouse, there was a closed circuit TV monitor which covered most of the State and County buildings in the area. Someone was supposed to be watching the various screens at all times. If any activity was noticed, it called for a determination of what was going on.

Guido's truck was parked so that only the front end was not in 'shadow' from the side of the Registry. This meant that three-quarters of it could not be seen on any TV screen.

The Registry had been built in 1955-56. Before that date, all records had been stored in the old Courthouse. Guido had watched construction and on several occasions had been inside the new Registry. He knew the layout as well as he knew the inside of the building in which he lived.

The First District Court of Barnstable, another relatively new building, lay at the far end of the extensive parking lot which served it, the Barnstable County Jail, the House of Correction, the old Courthouse and numerous places of business on Main Street.

Extension Services and Probate offices were reached through another parking lot on a side street. They were in the same building with the new Registry.

Anyone watching the unmoving TV monitors would, if able to stay awake, direct most of his attention to those screens where inmates would have to appear if attempting escape. Guido doubted if a dog or a cat or a drunk or a late walker would even be noticed on any of the other screens. In any case, he would not appear himself.

It was a simple matter to force the fire door at the top of the outside stairs. Leaving it ajar, Guido returned to the side street, Railroad Avenue, and waited fifteen minutes to see if any alarm had been set off. He was almost certain that nothing had been installed to protect these offices. There was no money in them, unless it was loose change. And except for a certain amount of office equipment - electrical typewriters, computers, calculators - there was nothing of value inside. Other than what he was after.

When he was sure it was safe, he returned and entered the Registry through the back way.

Title search is one of the lucrative games which lawyers play. Guido had been gouged when he bought the land where he built his house, and then he had been crunched again on the same property when he obtained the construction mortgage. He had talked with other buyers of real estate and had found out that every deed to real property is recorded in a book on a certain page of that book as soon as the sale goes through. When the papers have been recorded in that manner, the sale has been consummated.

But before you can buy a piece of land, or any building thereon, lawyers insist that they search all the deeds, back as far as there are records, in order to be certain that no one can come forward later and claim a right to the property. Guido could see that it was reasonable to make sure, before you laid down your money, that you were buying from the rightful owner. What he did not like was the way a single piece of property could be made into a pyramid of outrageous fees for an army of greedy lawyers simply because it changed hands again and again. Why was it necessary to do the same work over and over again?

What's more, he discovered that there are people in every Registry who do title searches for bankers and lawyers and they receive quite modest sums for their work. But when papers are passed, at the sale of the property, the fees for title search are usually a percentage of the price being paid for the entire property. The difference between the thirty or forty dollars paid to the person who actually does the work and the hundreds of dollars charged to the buyer by the lawyer, is nothing less than a scam. Guido felt no remorse about presenting a problem to persons he considered much less honest than he.

The books in which mortgages and related papers are recorded are unwieldy, to say the least. The older ones, in Barnstable, are about twenty-five by forty inches in size and weigh up to ten pounds each. The more recent ones are smaller but are still larger than the largest art books.

There are more than four thousand of these books in the Registry in the Barnstable County Registry of Deeds. That does not include any of the books of Grantors and Grantees or any of the many other documents available there.

Guido could not remove all the books from the Registry, nor did he want to, but he knew he could take enough to bring all real estate transactions in the county to a grinding halt - overnight.

He started with the older, larger books, taking them at random, carrying as many as possible. It was necessary to look down on the parking lot each time he was ready to take a load to the truck. If anyone had appeared he would have had to abandon everything.

Perspiration soaked his underwear even before he made his

first trip. He was wearing light gloves. It was cold that evening. The rear door of the truck was on a spring he had installed long ago so that with arms full he could step on a pedal under the fender and the door would swing open allowing him to step inside without having to set down his load. The door closed after him but didn't lock.

There was enough light from street lamps and from lights around the building so that he could see what he was doing without a flashlight. Except when he ran up or down the stairs there was little anyone could have noticed, even if someone had been watching.

Guido had calculated that he shouldn't spend more than an hour removing books. There was too much else to do before the night was over. With each trip his nervousness increased. He began taking the smaller, more recent tomes, as soon as he had about thirty of the older ones. He could carry many more of these. This selection, too, was made at random. When his hour was up he seemed not to have taken nearly enough to accomplish his purpose so he went back one more time, and then another.

Once, while he was upstairs, car lights swung across the room. It was a Barnstable cruiser circling the parking lot, the big one. Would it come around behind the Registry? Would the officer take a look at his truck? The door was closed but not locked. Suppose the cop saw that and decided to check. Guido held his breath while the cruiser went up past the jail and then returned to Main Street and disappeared.

When he was ready to take the last pile of books to the truck, Guido drew a note from his wallet and left it on the floor, just inside the door of the main entrance to the Registry. The lady who opened up in the morning would find it there.

He did his best to close the door he had forced so that no one would see it was damaged before opening time in the morning. He ran down the stairs for the last time. The final armful of books went into the back of the truck. He locked the door and went around to the side and got into the driver's seat. His heart was thudding as if he'd been swimming under water. He couldn't get his breathing under control.

What time was it? How much time did he have left?

He started the motor, praying that no one would hear, that the wind would cover the noise.

He drove out of the parking lot with no lights on and down to Main Street, then turned left and put the lights on and went as far as Old Jail Lane. He turned in there and extinguished the lights again and drove as cautiously as possible to a house he'd scouted weeks before whose owners wouldn't be around again until June.

The driveway went to the rear of the building where the truck would not be visible even if someone came along the road. Guido got out and easily opened the kitchen door by pushing his license against the catch as he had already done when he first checked out the house.

All the shades were down indoors so that even in full daylight no one could see inside the building. Guido off-loaded all the books, stacking them in the hallway so that even if there were a crack somewhere between window and shade, no one would see that anything was amiss from the outside.

He tore part of one page out of one book and folded it neatly and put it in a shirt pocket. Then he closed the kitchen door, got in the truck and drove to Old Rabbit Swamp Road and along it to Pine Street and back to where the truck had been parked before. He checked to be sure he had left nothing incriminating in it. Then he returned to his own quarters. As far as he knew, no one had seen or heard him.

He was shaking all over, as if overtaken by a terrible chill. He had never done anything even a little bit sneaky before in his entire life and here he had just spent three hours, or more, committing a serious crime.

He was unnerved. He stripped. He put the slip of paper on his bureau and threw all his clothes in the washer. After twenty minutes in the shower, under the hottest water he could stand, he finally got his body under control again. He lay down on his bed until dawn. Maybe he dozed a little. At his usual hour he was up, had breakfasted and was at work in his shop.

The lady who opened the Registry in the morning saw the note on the floor as she stepped inside. There were already three neatly attired attorneys waiting to get in. She spread her arms to keep them from passing her. "Something's wrong," she said. "Please wait."

She picked up the note. It was put together with words and letters cut from magazines or newspapers and pasted on a single sheet of paper.

THE BOOKS ARE SAFE ALL WILL BE RETURNED WHEN WE GET $25,000 HAVE THIS SUM READY IN USED TWENTIES BY FRIDAY DIRECTIONS WILL FOLLOW

The lady's eyes went to the racks where the books were kept. She saw many empty shelves. One of the lawyers noticed the fire door. "That door's been forced," he said.

"I think we must go back out," the lady said. "I'll lock up again and call the police. Our security man can stand outside the fire door until the authorities get here."

Guido heard the sirens and couldn't keep himself from breaking out in a sweat. He knew what they were for.

Within an hour Main Street was clogged with traffic as the word spread and people came from Sandwich and Yarmouth and Hyannis to find out first hand what had happened.

State police showed up quickly, along with local cops who were everywhere.

A customer came into the shop to pick up a sign.

"What is going on?" Guido asked.

"They ripped off the Registry," the customer said. "Took a lot of the stuff you need for looking up titles. Got in last night and got clean away. They want twenty-five grand to return the books."

Another customer had come in. "It won't work," he said. "There's microfilms of everything. Some bozo went to a lotta trouble for nothin'."

"Where's the microfilm?"

"How would I know? Prolly in a safe somewhere."

"Suppose they lost it?"

"Would be just like 'em."

"And even if they do have it, won't it cost a bundle to get it all printed out so you can use it?"

"So who cares? Except the tax payer, of course."

"That'll take time, though."

"Yeah, I guess it will. Might kinda mess up a lotta deals." The man started chuckling. "Think of all them schemin' lawyers standin' aroun' wettin' their pants with nothin' to do. No papers to shuffle. No fat fees to collect." He was beginning to enjoy himself.

"I had one charge me two hundred an' thirty-five bucks when I bought my house. I asked him what did he do for that. He looked down his nose at me and said somethin' about how title search was a critical an' demandin' professional endeavor. Bullshit. I come down here, found out where the Registry is, an old geezer sittin' by a window just watchin' told me where to start an' what to look for. In fifteen minutes I had it done. Nothin' to it. How long did it take him with his 'professional endeavor?' Two minutes?"

The two men settled accounts with Guido and as they left the second customer was saying: "I'll tell you a better one."

Guido knew about the microfilm. He'd heard talk of it long before. It was in a bank vault. He didn't know where. Maybe out of state. If the authorities decided to bring it in and use it they could refuse to pay any ransom at all. That was why he had kept the figure as low as he had. There was a point at which they would be obliged to refuse, but at somewhere in the neighborhood of twenty-five thousand they would find it faster and cheaper to pay. At least that was what he hoped.

Three days later, two men from the Barnstable police department came into the shop. One looked familiar. Sure enough. Guido had repaired a handsome colonial doorway on the man's house where carpenter ants had done serious damage. His name was Dugan. He remembered Guido.

"You park your truck behind the Registry every night, right?" the other detective asked.

"Yes," Guido said. "I had permission five, maybe six, years ago. The truck was liable to get hit being on the street all night in front of the shop."

"You notice anything unusual there when you parked it the night of the robbery?"

"No."

"Nobody hanging around?"

"I tried to remember, after I heard about the robbery. There are a couple of others who park there sometimes. I don't remember anything out of the ordinary."

"What time did you go to bed that night?"

"I always go to bed about eleven."

"Didn't hear anything that night?"

"Nothing wakes me once I go to sleep."

Dugan hadn't said anything so far. Now he apologized, it seemed. "We have to ask all these questions because whoever pulled off this job had to have a truck of some sort. Probably it took two people. They had to make some noise. Somebody is sure to have noticed something, or heard something, even though it happened late at night."

"I wish I could help you," Guido said. He lifted his shoulders and spread his palms in a typically Italian gesture.

Dugan was looking straight at him. "You didn't pull this one off yourself did you?"

He asked it as if he was joking. Was he?

"Mr. Dugan," Guido said, "I think you know me better than that."

He felt drops of perspiration running down his sides under his shirt. Both cops were staring at him.

Fortunately, another man came into the shop just then and asked the two detectives to come with him. They left.

Guido sat there with his heart pounding. For a second he had been sure that the two men had seen right through him. Cops have to be able to spot a guilty attitude. Still, even the most innocent person is likely to behave in a guilty manner when being quizzed by officers of the law. And maybe they hadn't noticed anything unusual. It was part of their profession to have that cop look, accusatory, all-knowing. Underneath, they were just ordinary men doing a job that was probably as dull and repetitive and as mired in red tape and endless reports as any job can be. If they retained any intuitive powers in a job like theirs it would be a miracle.

The most important thing, Guido thought, was not to worry. He must keep calm and go on with his life as if nothing were changed. He'd done the hardest part. Either he'd overlooked something, or someone somewhere had seen him or his truck and there was nothing he could do to change that, or everything had gone smoothly, no one had seen or heard anything, and he was home free. - Go about your business as you always have, he told himself. You don't know anything and nobody knows anything about what you have done.

The Saturday before, around noon, he had dropped a letter through the Cape Cod Only slot in the Hyannis Post Office. He'd managed to get in and out of there without speaking to anyone. He'd worn a coat he seldom wore and he'd kept a handkerchief to his mouth and nose most of the time, sniffling and blowing as if he had a cold. He'd only been in Hyannis for half an hour and had stopped at Bradfords for some finishing nails in order to make the trip seem legitimate - and innocent - if anyone ever asked.

The letter was addressed to Register Weeks, Registry of Deeds, Barnstable Village. The address was in block letters. The letter, once more put together from words cut out of a local newspaper, read as follows: "Do not show this to the police. We will know if you do. This Wednesday, at ten-thirty PM, get into your car, after painting a solid orange circle, six inches in diameter on the window on the passenger side. You will have the $25,000 with you in used unmarked bills in a plain paper bag. You may arm yourself if you wish. You may not have any kind of operating radio in the car. You will be alone in the car. No electronic tracking device or marker or other means of determining the position of your car or the money when delivered can be tolerated. You <u>must</u> understand that if one of us is apprehended, all material we hold will be destroyed.

"You will drive along the Mid-Cape highway, starting at exit 7 and going to exit 6. Leave the Mid-Cape there and go to Route 6A. Drive along it going east until you reach Willow Street. Turn right and go to the Mid-Cape and repeat. Keep circling until you see two beer bottles upright in the road. Stop and place the paper bag beside the bottles, off the road. Get back in your car and drive away and complete the circle two more times.

"If any vehicle seems to be following you, if there is any indication that any part of this route is being watched, if anything whatsoever makes us think you or the police or any other agents are trying in any way to intercept or trap us, the money and the records may both be lost. The recovery of what we hold, intact, depends entirely upon you."

The letter was part of a stack of mail on Mr. Weeks' desk when he entered his office after talking with the local police. They had taken the first note with them and they had examined the interior of the Registry as well as the forced door.

Weeks sat at his desk. There were more than forty people outside, mostly attorneys, hoping to get in to complete whatever business they had. Real estate brokers all over the Cape and Islands were phoning to find out how long it would be before they could count on doing business again. Several banks had already declared the situation intolerable.

When the Register picked up the ransom note he knew what it was immediately. His first impulse was to throw all responsibility on the police. He had already reached for the phone when he decided to read the letter and think it over first.

He went through the note carefully and then put it in his wallet. If he acted on his own, the whole matter might be settled over the week-end. This was not a kidnapping. No lives were endangered. The amount of money involved was not prohibitive. In fact, it was quite modest. If he sent for the microfilm and started reproducing all the records that had been stolen - and first he'd have to make a determination of that - the expense would probably exceed the amount being demanded. It would be disruptive. It would take longer. And the books themselves would be lost. They had considerable historical interest, at least the older volumes did. You could hardly put a dollar value on that.

Suppose he decided to try to raise the money? The county

wouldn't come up with it without legislative action. Who knows how long that could take? But a group of bankers and brokers...How about the lawyers, too? If everyone kicked in a certain amount...

He asked one of the women in the office to compile a list of the people phoning in who claimed they absolutely had to have access to the files without delay, as well as names of any others likely to be adversely affected by what had happened. Before the end of the afternoon he had a list of over sixty names. He set up a meeting for nine o'clock that evening with as many of these as could get there.

"We need to decide how to handle the ransom demand," he told each one he phoned. "Since this may affect you directly, I think you should have a say in the matter."

Fifty-three brokers, bankers and attorneys gathered in a courtroom in the old courthouse that night. No one from the media and no one from law enforcement was allowed in.

"This is a private matter," Weeks told those who were being excluded. "We intend to find out what the majority opinion is on a question that concerns us intimately."

When the doors were closed, Weeks announced that he had received the second ransom note and had instructions on delivery of the money.

"I will not reveal the contents of this note at this time," he said, "unless it is your wish to refuse payment. Knowing the terms gives me a lot more information than you have on which to make a judgement, but it is my view that even without knowing the details it would be wisest to pay up without attempting apprehension until afterwards.

"If I turn the note over to the police at this point, the person, or (more likely) persons, holding the records we so desperately need, will know within hours and will almost certainly destory what we might otherwise recover. If we refuse, we are faced with an expense virtually certain to exceed the amount now demanded. And no telling how long it will take to make available once more, everything that was available until just last week-end. I sincerely believe that the best and speediest way out of this mess is to pay."

Discussion was brief and one-sided. Twenty-five thousand dollars represented a trivial percentage of the total commissions, bank fees and lawyers' charges pending on deals which might die a-borning as things stood now. An entire industrial park was hung up on this theft. The bank involved in that enterprise had two million dollars allocated but resting in limbo while the final transaction was postponed. Three condominium complexes awaited closings. A foreign oil baron had agreed to purchase an oceanview estate. The novice broker responsible for that offer had had a heart attack and his wife was about to follow suit if the sale was not to be consummated. The oil baron didn't care.

In less than an hour, the twenty-five thousand was pledged and all present promised to keep mum. Weeks was to turn all the notes into cash at the Bank of Boston, in Hyannis, the following morning. A few of those present had wanted to see the thief, or thieves, denied such easy gain, but among businessmen, money under the table, or at the back door, or as nominal lubricant, is routine - simply another deductible cost. Forget it.

Word did get out that those present at the meeting had decided to pay, but since the note found on the Regsitry floor had said to have the money ready by Friday, and since only Weeks knew the terms of the second note, the various investigators working on the case continued quizzing Registry employees and checking door-to-door all roads away from the Registry to find out if anyone had seen, or heard, or noticed anything the night of the theft.

They were certain a truck had been used. They tended to believe that at least two persons had worked together to remove the books. They suspected an inside job. But the slim leads they accumulated all led nowhere.

As for the ransom note - the only one in the hands of the authorities - analysis showed that the Cape Cod Times had been the source of the words and letters used. There were no prints and anyone could have had paper and paste of the types used by the perpetrator.

Phones in the Registry were tapped to cover the possibility that instructions on delivery might come by that route. Two technicians were on duty there twenty-four hours a day, ignorant of the fact that the instructions had already been delivered by the United States Postal Service.

No watch had been put on Register Weeks.

Wednesday evening Guido ate supper and went to bed early. He left the lights on. Usually, if not working, he would read until about eleven. His habits seldom varied. He dozed an hour and then woke up, before his alarm went off. It was a quarter of eleven. He turned out the lights then, as if he were going to seleep. He dressed in dark clothes - dirty sneakers, navy-blue corduroy pants, a wool shirt and black turtle-neck sweater, a knitted hat and brown gloves.

He went out the back way, staying in the shadows as much as possible, and made his way to Railroad Avenue. There was no one around at that hour. The short distance he had to walk on Main Street was the only dangerous stretch where someone could have noticed him. It was deserted. He walked up Railroad Avenue and along Old Hot Bottom Road to where it intersected Phinney's Lane. Some of the way, he cut through back yards. He had long ago picked out a spot from which he could observe the Mid-Cape highway. It was a wooded section.

The Register's car went by, traveling about thirty-five miles an hour. The orange circle on the window was easy to spot from a considerable distance. Guido checked his watch to see how long it would take for the car to make a complete circuit, making sure no other vehicle was following.

Traffic was very light - a big semi every now and then and an occasional car traveling faster than the speed limit.

Guido was confident that his instructions had been followed and that no cops were aware of what was going on. The two green beer bottles were where he had hidden them two weeks earlier. He let the car cruise by once more before timing it and then setting the bottles in the road, not way out where they might get hit, but far enough so that they would be obvious to anyone looking for them. He had timed it perfectly.

Inside the car, Weeks was getting more nervous every minute. He'd lost count of the number of times he'd gone around the route. It was clear that whoever the pick-up man (or woman) was, that one would have to be watching to see if there was any sign of police intervention. Still, there were limits to how many times he could circle without losing his mind.

The money was on the seat at his right in tight packets in an ordinary shopping bag. He hadn't brought a weapon. He hated guns. Anyway, he couldn't see why he might need one.

When his lights glinted on two bottles in the road, he pulled over almost with relief. He got out and carried the bag to the edge of the road. There was no sign of anyone anywhere, yet there were eyes on him. He could almost feel them.

As quickly as he could, he got back into the car and drove away. He almost forgot he was to circle two more times. He did that at high speed and went home and fell into bed, more exhausted than he'd been in years.

Guido picked up the bag of money as soon as the car was out of sight. He threw the bottles into the shrubbery and moved quickly into the woods. The remains of a stone wall, five hundred yards away, was his destination. He had picked out the wall at the same time he had hidden the two bottles. With a trowel he had enlarged a cavity under a sizable stone that lay in a bed of pine needles and he had put an empty two quart honey jar there.

It only took a minute to lift the stone, fill the jar with the money, screw the lid on tight, put the jar inside the paper bag and bury it under a little dirt. With the stone back in place no one was likely to notice anything had ever been disturbed.

Guido then returned home by almost the same route he had taken earlier. When he was once more safely inside his own apartment, he put the dark clothes away and went to bed. He lay on his bed smiling. He'd done it. He went to sleep and for once didn't wake up until after the sun had risen.

The only thing left to do was to let someone know where the stolen goods were hidden. He wrote the address in block letters across the partial page he had taken from one of the books on Sunday night. He put this in an envelope, sealed it, and wrote the name and home address of the Register on the envelope. Later in the day, in Hyannis, he dropped the letter in the Cape Cod Only slot at the Post Office. It was a busy time of day. He didn't run into anyone he knew. He stopped at a paint supply store for some black enamel he needed and went back to his shop.

Guido was just about certain there was no way he could be tied to the theft. The money should be safe where it was hidden, unless that piece of land were sold and developed. But he'd know about that in time to go get it. There was a chance that the bills had been marked or the serial numbers noted. It would not be wise to spend them too soon or to spend them locally. That wasn't part of his plan anyway. He was a little worried that he hadn't had a chance to inspect them before revealing the hiding place of the books, but it was inconceivable that Weeks would have done anything like short-changing him, or using phony money. He would have assumed that the thief, or thieves, would check the money immediately.

Guido's third note was delivered Friday morning. The Register didn't see it until he went home at six. The message was perfectly clear. He drove to the house on Old Jail Lane and found it closed and empty. He even tried the doors, but they were closed and locked. He drove to the Registry and phoned the police.

"We can't just break in," they said. "You need a court order to enter there."

"I'll get one," the Register said. "Come here and meet me at the rear door of the Old Courthouse."

Judge Augustus Wagner was finishing some paper work when the Register walked in on him. He'd followed the case with interest. Not often did a robbery involve only books. In fact, this might be the first time it had ever happened. He was happy to sign the order. He came along, too, to see if the books would be there.

Somehow, a reporter from the Times and a photographer joined them. What a sense of smell, or something, those guys have! There were two Barnstable cops in a cruiser, the judge in his own car, the Register in his, and two plain clothes men in a new Chevvy. They drove to Old Jail Lane and one of the officers opened the rear door just the way Guido had. An hour later all the books were back in the Registry, and after another hour all were back in place. The torn page was eventually framed and put on a wall in the Register's office with a full account of the week's (Weeks) proceedings.

In no time, the investigation, though not exactly dropped, became a desultory effort. Sympathy seemed to be more with the malefactor (or malefactors) than with the victims. When the men who had put up the twenty-five thousand sought reimbursement, a howl of protest went up. Hadn't they acted on their own in defiance of official procedure? Weren't they, perhaps, even guilty of malfeasance? In any case, they had acted out of self-interest and for personal gain and had already reaped any reward to which they might conceivably have been entitled.

Dugan came to see Guido one day when things had pretty much quieted down.

He set one haunch on a work bench and stared at Guido. "How you doin', Mr. Bussatti?" he asked.

Guido had been expecting him. He didn't stop work, but he looked over at the detective and said: "All right."

"Keepin' busy?"

"There is always work to do, Mr. Dugan."

"I been thinkin' about you," Dugan said. "We have several things to go on, you know. I'm referring to the matter of the records that got removed from the Registry, of course. A very neat job. Meticulous, you might say. The sort of thing somebody who does careful well-planned precise work would do. You know what I mean?"

Guido was making measurements for a thrift shop sign that had been ordered recently. He had a rough drawing in front of him tacked onto the wall and was deciding layout on a plank before him. He set aside his tools and turned to face Dugan. "I think I understand you," he said.

There was the smell of fresh-cut pine in the shop and Dugan was breathing it in. "Nice in here," he said. "Restful. The kinda place you can keep still in and think about anything, figure out how to get a thing done right."

He filled his lungs and let the air out slowly. Then, looking into Guido's eyes, he said: "The crook, or crooks, had to use a truck. They had to be in Hyannis, at least one of them, on Saturday, before the crime, when the note was mailed that was delivered to the Registry on Monday. And they had to go there, or be there, again on Thursday when the final note was mailed to the Register's house. The same person, or persons, was (were) very busy in the early hours of Monday and for a while around midnight on Wednesday."

He sat staring at Guido. There was a hint of a smile on his face. Guido kept silent.

"No comment?" Dugan asked.

"What do you want me to say?"

"I thought you would say: I deny having had anything to do with the theft from the Registry."

Guido shrugged. "I deny having had anything to do with the theft from the Registry."

"Hmmm. Where were you at the crucial times."

"You know, Mr. Dugan, that I've already answered all these questions. I was sleeping at night and I often go to Hyannis for supplies."

"So you could have mailed those notes."

"But I didn't."

"Your panel truck would have been just the right size for the job that was done."

"More Cape Codders have trucks than cars."

"We know that," Dugan said. "It makes it tough."

Guido was almost relaxed. He wondered at how calm he was. Then he realized it was due to the repetition. Dugan, and others, had taken him over this same territory at least three times now. They couldn't prove a thing and he had all the answers down pat. At least so far...

"Tell me something, Guido." Dugan had both feet on the floor and was only leaning against the bench now. "Ever since your wife divorced you, what do you do for, you know, female company?"

Guido hesitated. "That's a personal matter," he said.

"I was just thinkin' that if you had been in the arms of Mary, say, instead of Morpheus, you'd be off the hook."

"Am I on the hook, as you say?"

"You are a very slippery fish, Guido. That's for sure. What about Edith?"

This hadn't been covered before. "Is that something I am obliged to tell you?"

"Just wonderin'," Dugan said. "How about it?"

"I hope you will do nothing to compromise the lady."

"Don't you see her anymore?"

"Only rarely now. We are still friends."

Dugan shook his head. "You wanna know what really bugs me, Guido?"

"What is it that really 'bugs' you, Mr. Dugan?"

"It's that note. The second one. Weeks should have given it to us right away, instead of after the fact, but we've got it now an' I've read it over an' over. I asked about six people to write me a ransom note to set up a drop along those lines. Nobody. I mean nobody at all, could do it as neatly or as briefly. Here you are. A foreigner. Could you write a note like that?"

"I don't know," Guido said. "I never had the occasion."

Dugan started to pull his coat on again. It was a cold day outside. "You got style, Guido," he said. "I like you. I think you're our man, though. Someday I'd like to know for sure. Hey, you goin' back to Italy soon?"

"When I save enough money to set myself up in a gallery in Arezzo, then I'll go."

"With twenty-five G's you could go tomorrow."

"I have about eight thousand in my savings account now. When it gets to fifteen, I'll go."

"I guess I hope you make it. How do you say 'Good Luck' in Italian?"

"*In bocc'al lupo*...Into the mouth of the wolf."

"That's an odd way to put it."

"Don't you Americans say...Break a leg?"

"It's not quite the same. Or maybe it is. I won't forget you, Guido Bussatti."

"I won't ever forget you either, Mr. Dugan."

In the months that followed, Guido worked as he always had. It could be that he devoted a little more time than usual to his sculpture. A few pieces sold. He could have marketed any number of figures of squirrels and rabbits, but it was in abstract forms that his interest lay and just cranking out cute animals for an indiscriminate public would have disturbed him.

Each piece of wood awaited its own treatment. Often, he kept a log or a plank for months before intuition told him what should be done with it. He was aware of activity in some obscure part of himself, a subconscious stirring which required its own time before surfacing, before he "knew" what he was called upon to create.

If he was impatient to be gone, it didn't show. He had deep ties in America after spending so many years here. A great many people knew and liked him.

Whenever Guido sent sculpture to Italy, the agent ribbed him about spending good money to export stuff that would never get sold. The agent was a Greek who had lived on Cape Cod even longer than Guido had. He claimed he had no desire to return to the land of his birth, but Guido suspected that he was kidding himself. There was envy in his tone. His derision hid a secret longing.

In the course of the last summer, before he left, Guido drove to Framingham to say goodbye to Luciana. He hadn't seen her for over ten years. The address he had was an old one and when he parked in front of the house he saw nothing to indicate that

Luciana was still there.

The small split-level ranch on the quarter acre lot was like a hundred thousand others in Boston suburbs - two rhododendruns in front, a picture window, shake siding (dark red in this case), a lamppost by the sidewalk with petunias at its base.

He pushed a button by the door and heard two-tone chimes ring inside. A moment later the door opened. His ex-wife was forty pounds heavier. Her one-time resplendent black hair was bleached blond with dark roots barely visible. She still had a lovely smile. The generous mouth was unchanged and the perfect teeth also.

"Yes?" she said. She hadn't recognized him with the neatly trimmed beard he had cultivated lately.

"Hello, Luciana," he said.

Her smile faded. "It's you. I thought you had left the country."

"I am leaving in a few months. I wanted to say goodbye to you. Are you going to ask me in?"

She stepped aside so he could enter. They went into a living room furnished in exactly the style that had been responsible for their first dispute.

"I'm known as Lucy Bussy now," she said as they sat down. "I changed my name after the divorce. I'd prefer to have you refer to me that way if you mention me anywhere."

He almost asked her why she had changed her name, then realized he didn't need to. It was one more part of her repudiation of a heritage she felt demeaned her. Had Peter changed his name too? They hadn't said so, but he wasn't Pierino anymore.

"So how are you, Lucy? You look well."

"I'm fine. No thanks to you. I've put on a few pounds."

"You haven't remarried?"

"That would relieve your mind, I suppose."

"I'd be glad to know you are happy. That's all."

"And marriage is happiness?"

"It wasn't for us, but I believe it can be."

"What about you? Have you remarried?"

"I have never considered it. You are still my wife, in the eyes of the Church."

"Don't get the idea that means anything to me."

"I won't. I think back, though, to when you and I first met and it is hard to believe that we moved so far apart. Do you ever remember those times?"

"What's to remember? I was young and stupid. I didn't have any idea of what was important."

"You were young and beautiful, Luciana..."

"Call me Lucy."

"You were young and very beautiful, Lucy. And you believed in love. As I did. Maybe we were wrong to expect it to last. But it was important then. It still is."

She had taken a cigarette from a pack on a side table. She lit it and then blew smoke at him.

"Still the same dreamer you always were, eh Guido? Has anything changed? Are you still the little sign painter in the cramped dreary shop, working from sun-up to sundown and dreaming? What are your dreams now - besides this nonsense about love? Will you go back to Italy and get famous?"

"I don't know," Guido said. He looked down at his hands, those hands that had worked on a thousand signs, that had become a sculptor's hands, hands that had once held the young body of the woman before him. "I don't know if I will ever be famous. It's not likely. But I'll be going home soon and I hope to have a small gallery there for some of my wood carving."

"You're a wood carver now! Well! No more signs? Have you gotten rich?"

"No. But I have saved enough money to be able to go where I hope to find peace once more."

"Another dream! Peace! Peace is in the grave."

He raised his eyes to meet hers again. "You have never seen the Tuscan countryside, Luci...Lucy, the terracing on the hillsides, the ripe wheat standing platinum white in the fields, the olive groves and the vineyards. There is peace there."

"And after forty years you think your Italy hasn't changed?"

"For two thousand years it didn't change."

They looked at each other. She would never believe him, and there could be some truth in what she suggested. There had been changes during his absence. The land, worked for millenia by simple peasant people, had overnight been abandoned. Factory jobs, the lure of the city, a regular pay check and access to material goods, had drawn the younger people away from the earth to which, for so long, they had been bound. Franca had written of it. She too had taken a job in a *fabbrica*, a place that manufactured sewing machine parts. Viticulture was no longer in the hands of thousands of different individuals, but was being taken over by huge combines. The same was true for the olive oil that had once been different for every owner of a hundred trees. He might not find the tranquillity he remembered when he returned. Home might not be home anymore. He was going anyway.

"Do you need anything, Lucy?" he asked.

"I need everything. What do you think?"

"I mean really need. Not just want."

"I've got a roof over my head. I eat regularly. What else is there, according to you?"

"If you should ever run into real hardship, you might let me know." He gave her the address he would have in Castiglion Fiorentino.

She took the piece of paper he handed her and dropped it on the side table next to her cigarettes. "You'll starve," she said. "I know you. You'll live in an unheated room, like all the other old timers in the old country. You'll whittle your fingers off and freeze in the winter and roast in the summer."

"We have a big apartment, Lucy. My mother and sister still live in the apartment in which I was born. It will have a forced hot water heating system soon after I get there."

"You didn't mention your father. Did he die?"

"Yes. What about your father?"

"Mine too. He got in a fight and was stabbed. He bled to death. He would have lived if someone had taken him to the hospital right away. Then Paolino was caught carrying cigarettes from one state to another to avoid taxes so he lost all the trucks. Marcello and Ma are still there in the North End. Marcello is still in the same household loan affice."

"Do you ever see them?"

"What for?"

"I liked your mother. If you see her I wish you would tell her I remember her with genuine affection. But maybe I'll write her. She would like that, I think."

"Sure, why not. You might turn into a writer and get rich that way too."

A sense of lost opportunity came over Guido, and sadness. "Do you want to know something, Lucy?" he said. "Life can be very good if you don't demand too much of it."

Did she hear him at all? She didn't answer. There was something greedy and spoiled in her that would always be looking for more. It was the other face of the young woman's irrepressible anticipation of things joyous and magical, a childish faith in a sunlit future. That was part of what had drawn him to her years ago, but he had not foreseen that he could never fulfill her expectations.

He didn't stay much longer. It was clear that they would start to argue if he did. He said his farewells and left and realized he had never found out what she did to support herself. Did Marcello send her money? Was there insurance money from her father's death? Had she invested the money she got from the sale of the house in Barnstable? Maybe she had someone on the string who helped her out. It didn't much matter. She had a roof over her head, as she had pointed out, and enough to eat. Too much, evidently.

He drove back to the Cape slowly, thinking about how much they had missed but relieved in the knowledge that she lacked nothing essential. If there were intangibles which might have served her, she was unaware of them.

As the time for leaving approached, he took more and more long walks. He carried a backpack, as he had on his first trip to the Cape. One day he went to the place where the money was hidden. He lifted the stone and withdrew the jar. He put it in his knapsack. That evening he checked it. There was no sign that any bills had been marked or that there was any pattern of serial numbers. There were exactly twenty-five thousand dollars in used twenties in the jar. It made an awkward bundle. He'd have to give a lot of thought to how he would get it into Italy. But by then all investigations of the theft had long since been filed. There'd be time.

At a lumber yard he ran into Dugan once.

"Still playin' it cool, Mr. Bussatti?"

"I am still working and saving."

"I wonder if I was wrong about you."

"We all make mistakes sometimes," Guido replied.

Dugan muttered something and started to walk away. Then he turned just as Guido was about to start walking. "*In bocc'al lupo,*" he said.

"Break a leg," Mr. Dugan."

Their eyes met and each waved at the other. It was not only a wave of farewell, there was mutual respect in it too.

Guido shipped his personal belongings and most of his hand tools to Italy. In another crate, he sent his remaining abstracts. He sold everything else he owned for enough cash to pay air fare to Milano.

There were three months left on his lease, but the landlord let him off without asking for payment. It was spring and Guido was leaving everything in perfect repair. The building would be rented for more money than ever before in a matter of days. The landlord told Guido he'd miss him, but it was clear that his mind was more on the increased rent he'd soon be getting than on the departure of someone he'd known for almost four decades.

Others said goodbye in the same perfunctory way. It was disconcerting how so many years came down to a handshake and a slap on the back. Shopkeepers, the mailman, the barber, old customers - "Hey, take care of yourself," and back into the moment. His going meant little more to them than his arrival had when they had never seen him before. Perhaps less.

He had never gone to see Lance Bragdon again. A card once, at Christmas, had indicated Lance's marriage was on the rocks.

Guido took the bus to Boston. There was time to kill. He walked around Beacon Hill and the North End without running into anyone he knew. The streets looked drab and dirty to him.

He looked for himself there, the young man in his twenties so full of enthusiasm and dreams - those dreams Luciana so denigrated. - Where did you go? *Dove sei andato?* he asked himself. But in the dank alleyways of the Hill, Guido, in his sixties, couldn't find his other self.

He got on the subway at Park Street and transferred and reached Logan. His suitcase contained only a few clothes, toilet articles, presents for his sister and mother.

The monster jet took off and before turning onto course the coast of America had been left behind.

Guido had never flown before. He found it exhilarating. They were above the clouds in minutes. A sea of white lay beneath them and except for the drone of the giant motors there was nothing to tell him they were moving. They were a speck of insignificant matter suspended in space.

In Milano, in Customs, then on the train, his ears were filled with the sound of Italian again, his native tongue. What a voluble demonstrative people they were, these of his own land, loud and uninhibited, always acting a part, in no way related to those sheathed silent guarded Americans he had met in New York City so long ago!

And the accents! The dialects! Here was a man near him speaking *Veneto* and Guido could not understand more than an occasional word. Near that one was a pair arguing in *Milanese*, French words contorted into Italian shapes.

"*Perchè sorride, Signore?*" asked a short dark man who stood in the train corridor next to Guido... "Why are you smiling?"

"*Perchè oggi torno a casa,*" Guido answered... "Because today I am coming home."

"*Cioè?*" the man asked, not understanding... "That is?"

But Guido just kept smiling. He didn't want to consume his feelings with mere words. He felt himself still flying, still off the ground, clouds cushioning him and white sunlight intense on everything he saw.

Franca met him at the station. She was thinner, bonier, and her hair was gray, but he would have known her anywhere. Her height and her long heavy-lobed ears, her reserved manner, set her apart. They embraced awkwardly. She had not been prepared for the little brother who was suddenly a gentleman of a certain age with an alien aspect and cagy eyes.

He learned that his mother hadn't been able to come to meet him. After all, she was in her eighties now and her eyesight - it was glaucoma - had deteriorated. She could barely distinguish light from dark.

A friend of Franca's drove them to Castiglione and dropped them at their door.

They went upstairs.

La Minca was straight and spry and, except for her blindness, seemed little older than her daughter. She kissed Guido and let old hands move over his hair and face, his neatly trimmed beard, his suit. Strong fingers clasped his arms.

"You are in good health?" she asked, in Italian.

"Excellent," he replied.

"I feared I would never see you again."

"I am back now, Mamma. I won't leave again."

His former room was his once more. The sculpture he had sent from America was stored in what had been his father's room. All his father's tools were there, together with the few books Piero had always valued, and some of his work. His shop, on the street, had been emptied and done over and then rented to a baker.

Guido arranged to have a modern heating system installed in the apartment. There would be no more huddling in the kitchen all winter to keep warm. He bought a modern gas stove and a big refrigerator which intimidated the women at first, but soon made them grateful for the convenience it afforded them. He found workmen to put in an American style bathroom where the old *gabinetto* had been.

Meanwhile, he scoured Arezzo until he found a location he wanted for his gallery. The rent would be high, but he was filled with confidence. His Social Security check, in dollars, was enough to cover almost all their expenses. There were still seven thousand dollars of his own savings in the Bank of America. And there were twenty-five thousand more.

When the crates of his possessions came from the States, he had to go to the station and meet the Customs people there. The crates were opened. The inspectors asked about some of the items and lifted out a few carvings.

"*E questo qui?*...And this?" one demanded, eyeing a shape that could have been a nude female torso but lacked any conclusive details.

"*Sono scultore*...I am a sculptor," Guido stated, giving himself just enough importance to make the inspector uncertain. "I have a gallery here in Arezzo. I hope you will come to see my work. All these carvings, which were on display in America until recently, will be showing in my studio here within a week."

There were five abstracts in the larger crate, each about two feet high, with base. The two inpectors took them out and hefted them, looked at them and shook their heads as if to say that Art was not what it used to be. Then they repacked the contents and let them be trucked to the gallery.

Some days later, Guido opened the crates again. The gallery was spacious with a deep front room on the street and a second room behind it where Guido could work.

The carving the inspector had first eyed was titled "The Secret." Guido set it on its side on his bench and with a three-inch circle bit in a power drill he cut into the center of the base until he reached a depth of one and a half inches. He turned off the drill and cautiously removed the cylinder of wood he had cut from the base of the statue. Inside, in tight rolls, wrapped in plastic, was the money. Guido removed it, hid it, and glued a flat second base onto the statue.

Little by little, over the months, he exchanged dollars for lire, with different parties. It was well known that he had lived in America for many years. There was no reason to question the fact that he might have a certain amount of United States currency to dispense with. Eventually he was able to purchase his gallery. There was still a little money left over.

He bought a small car so he could get back and forth from the studio and so he could travel to Florence and to other cities where his work was slowly gaining favor.

Locally, people began referring to him as Dottore Bussatti, bestowing an honorary imaginary degree upon him. He was not displeased.

One day, as he prepared to close the gallery in the late afternoon, two young women entered. They were Americans. They were whispering together and looking at him. Then they walked over to him and one said: "Hello, Grandpa."

He stared, not daring to believe it. "You are Lucy?" he asked. "And Maggie?"

They nodded.

He wanted to hug and kiss them, but they were fully grown and he feared they might not want him to do so.

"How wonderful!" he said. "How did you find me?"

"You're very well known, Grandpa."

Lucy was the elder. She was darker than her sister, more self-assured, but Maggie, with her strawberry-colored hair and her sideways look was going to drive men wild.

"We wanted to see you," Lucy said, "and we thought it was time to get away from home and see part of Europe. So we saved our money and came on a thirty-day tour of Italy. We have train passes so we can go everywhere."

"Did you remember that I lived near Arezzo?"

"Mom did. She said to go to Castiglion Fiorentino, but when we asked where it was and said we were looking for Signor Bussatti, people said: 'You mean the famous *scultore*?'"

"Then we were afraid you would be too important to want to see us." Maggie was the one to add this. She was half-kidding, half-flattering. You could see that she was going to be a woman to keep men off balance all her life. They'd never be certain what she really thought of them.

"I am not important at all," Guido said. "And even if I were, nothing would be more important to me than to have you two come to see me."

They spent four days with him. They met La Minca, their great grandmother, and Franca. Guido drove them to Florence for a day, and to Assisi, and to Bologna. Their Italian was good enough to get them what they wanted and it was improving swiftly. They were especially interested in painting and sculpture, and they could not get enough of Italian cooking or the desserts.

"If Grandma Lucy ate the way we do she'd be the size of the Duomo in Florence," Maggie said. "But we don't even gain an ounce."

"How is Luciana?" Guido asked. He had written her twice since leaving the States but she had never answered.

"She's all right," Lucy answered. "She complains about everything, but she's into anti-nukes and feminism and keeps busy. She's tough, you know."

Guido was surprised. He'd never thought of her as tough. Was she? Maybe so. Or maybe that was a female characteristic, to be tough, whereas men, who were expected to be that way, were quite often the opposite - sentimental, visionary.

"And your father?" he asked, another time. "How is my son? Can you tell me anything about him?"

The two girls exchanged a look.

"That's one of the big reasons we came to see you, Grandpa," Lucy said. "The one and only time Mom saw you she was terribly upset by the way Dad treated you. She said she thought you were a good and kind person and that Dad was awfully wrong to send you away. He still seems to have a kind of resentment about you. We don't understand it. But when we told him we wanted to try to find you so we could meet you, now that we're not children anymore, he told us we were right to look you up. 'Go ahead,' he said. 'It will make him happy.'"

Each year, for *Capo d'anno*...New Years, Guido sent a card to Dugan. It was always a photograph of one of his recent wood carvings and the message always read: "I have not forgotten you, Mr. Dugan. Happy New Year."

And each year on Independence Day, Dugan sent Guido a card showing fireworks bursting in a black sky and forming a giant question mark.

The year Guido died - he knew it was to be his last - he sent a photo to Dugan. It was a photograph of a piece he had never sold and which had always remained in the same position in the center of his gallery. There was no message that time on the delicately tinted photograph of "The Secret."

The Arno still runs muddy and brown in the spring and gray-green and clear with melting snows earlier. Cypresses still walk down the hills of Tuscany in stately columns. They stand around the country cemetery where Guido was laid to rest. In the end, he came home.